Mass Casualty

Author: Derek Adam

This book is a work of fiction. Many of the characters, places, and incidents are inspired by true events and locations, and are fictitious products of the author's imagination. Any resemblance to actual events, locales, or persons, living or dead, is entirely coincidental.

Copyright © 2017 Derek Adam

All Rights Reserved

No part of this book may be reproduced, copied, or transmitted in any form or by any means, electronic or mechanical without the expressed permission of the author.

This book is licensed for your personal enjoyment only. Thank you for respecting the hard work of this author.

Cover design provided by AWT Cover Designs

Editing provided by: Jillian Elizabeth/Jilly's Polished Proofs

From the Author

While writing Mass Casualty, I drew on my experience working EMS in the Metro Detroit area and northern Michigan. While that career wasn't a long one in the grand scheme of my life, I saw my fair share of miracles, mundane calls, and terrible things. I lost people close to me as well.

Most of that was locked away as a means of coping. It wasn't until the writing of this book that I began unlocking doors and revisiting things – both good and bad. Most of the encounters that take place in this book are inspired by true life events. Revisiting those memories brought the realization that even years later, they still have teeth. I wrestled with an overwhelming amount of grief and emotion in processing it all over again.

The men and women who work in the healthcare industry have a thankless job, are tremendously undercompensated, and often struggle to cope with the things they experience on a daily basis. Those experiences get locked away and hopefully forgotten, others are used to strengthen resolve.

Many simply cope through adopting twisted, dark humor to get them through.

Regardless of how they cope, it changes them. Every one of them. There is not a man or woman alive who works in healthcare that is not changed by what they experience.

It's most difficult to think about the ones we lose, who go too soon. Sometimes it's by accident. Sometimes the ability to cope is broken, and they make the ultimate choice to leave this world behind them.

If you work in this industry, don't hesitate to utilize available resources for counseling. Talk to someone. Your partner, friend, spouse, family, counselor – anyone. Locking those memories behind closed doors is only temporary.

And we've lost too many of you already.

Alicia-

My darling, my dearest, my queen. For the countless hours you tended to the castle while I wrote endlessly. For all the unquestioned support, following gleefully behind me as I led us blindly into one adventure after another. My love for you will last a lifetime, and beyond, in the hearts of the wonderful children you've gifted me.

Jill-

My unicorn. My Eleanor. The woman who is my girlfriend but doesn't know it yet. Not a day goes by that I am not thankful for finding you in my life. I owe you more than you know, and more than you'll ever take credit for. Without you this book never would have happened. Your endless encouragement has changed my life more than you can imagine.

My Children-

Thank you for looking at me like a hero when your eyes fall on me. You lift me up. I pray I have the strength to lead you and provide you with a better life than I had. Never let anyone tell that you can't do something (except your mother and I. Stop jumping on the god damn couches.)

Scott-

You are the Hunter to my Badger. Forever and ever, babe.

My Beta Readers-

For those who took the time to read the early versions and provide feedback on my first book, I owe you a tremendous debt of gratitude. Thank you for helping me sculpt this terrific story. There's a piece of each of you buried deep, and there it shall stay.

To my brothers and sisters on and off the road, and those who didn't make it… thank you for the sacrifices you make every day. Thank you for giving your mind, body, and spirit to the job. Both here and gone, you'll always have a place in my heart.

Mass Casualty Incident

"Any incident in which emergency medical services resources, such as personnel and equipment, are overwhelmed by the number and severity of casualties."

Chapter One - Old Wounds

"You know you're gonna kill yourself, right?" I pointed toward the garishly-colored can in Hunter's hand. He was in the process of sucking the life from another comically-oversized energy drink. He stared at me with mocking, wide eyes, gulping loudly with each guarana-infused chug.

"That's like...your third drink. Seriously. Your heart is going to exp-" I was cut off by a wagging finger as he drained the last drop, shaking the can over his mouth.

"Ooooh, that shit's gooooood," he spoke, the last word riding a deep belch as he crushed the can before throwing it over his shoulder into the back of the ambulance. "And that's number five today, bitch. I am all that is man."

"That shit is gross, and you're going to give yourself an arrhythmia. Why'd you throw that back there, I don't want that rattling around on a call." I thumbed toward the back of the rig. "Go clean that shit up."

"Relax Badger. I'm up next call anyway, I'll throw it away. Fuck, man. What's up your ass?"

He was right, he was up to tech the next call. I handled the last three patients, actually. I didn't like driving when we're stationed downtown. Every time I drive a shift here, shit always hits the fan. Work twice as hard for the same pay with the added risk of getting shot because some asshole wants your drug box.

Fuck this post, and this casino.

"I *hate* working this fucking post, Hunter. You know that." I didn't want to be there. It had nothing to do with Logan Hunter. He was the only thing that made this car bearable. He was a stupid ass, but he was my stupid ass.

Working with Hunter is a bonus because he's loyal, pretty good looking, and he's got a healthy dose of goofus. The women flock to him on shift. It's like having an adorable puppy with bright green eyes and a shaved head.

He's also brilliant, and one hell of a medic. The only one I'll ride with in the entire company. If Hunter is sick, then I'm sick. I don't roll with anyone else.

"I try not to think about it, Bobbie." I watched him shrug out an apology from the corner of my eyes. My focus had gone to another flurry of activity on the street ahead of where our ambulance was stationed outside the Pegasus casino in the heart of Greek Town.

It wasn't a bad post. Most of the pedestrian traffic was tourists, and there were always some Detroit PD close by. Occasional mugging, fighting, and other routine shit.

Sometimes, someone catches a knife.

Or a bullet.

Among the pedestrian traffic growing outside the entrance I could see two guys swinging at each other.

Surprise.

Young black guys, dressed for the hood, fighting like assholes. Probably over something stupid. Despite the growing crowd, there were still plenty of people wandering by as if nothing happened.

2

They were just too distracted by the glow of the casino lights and restaurants that sat huddled together in Greek Town. Despite the fact that it was almost midnight, there was enough light pollution here to make it seem like day time.

I wish I could be as oblivious to the fighting. These two idiots were gonna get someone hurt.

I didn't expect to treat them though. No.

The ones I worried about were the people hanging closely to the edge of the fight, trying to capture video of their very own YouTube moment. A surprising number of people set their morals aside for a bit of viral internet fame.

Those bystanders were always the ones who got hurt.

"That guy's getting knocked the fuck out." Hunter jabbed his finger at the window control, the sound of the casino nightlife filling the front of the ambulance as he stuck his head out "Hey, you guys mind? We're trying not to work tonight!"

He pulled his head in and settled back into the passenger seat. "Assholes."

We both chuckled then went silent as the Detroit PD rolled up with its lightbar spinning, letting out a couple chirps from its siren.

"Here we go. Popo." I grinned at Hunter and he laughed. He took a lot of delight in seeing "hoods" get collared. His word, not mine.

I couldn't give two shits, really. I held a general dislike for people in general, but appreciated the herd mentality and desire to stupidly injure themselves.

They kept me gainfully employed.

The crowd that had gathered in the street ahead of our rig broke suddenly, with people scattering in every direction, driven by the sound of gunshots ringing out. Hunter sputtered a curse and sunk down low in the passenger seat. I counted four… five… six rapid shots.

It was hard to see who was shooting, or what they were shooting at, but I imagine it had something to do with DPD showing up.

Someone didn't want to go to jail.

I didn't even flinch initially.

After all these years I've seen a lot of shit, especially gunshots. I'd worked in the D so many times it would surprise me more to have a week go by without a gunshot wound.

Two more shots rang out and I glanced to Hunter. He had managed to cram the entirety of his skinny fuckin body down on the floor in front of his seat. His small, compact frame was ideal for turtling.

Me on the other hand…

More shots fired. This time immediately followed by the sound of glass shattering as the windshield in front of me fractured. I doubled over, trying to compress my 6'2" frame as much as possible behind the dash.

Another round penetrated the windshield and I felt glass as it rained into the cab of the ambulance around us.

"Goddammit!" I clenched my eyes tight and tried to get even smaller. My foot slid and mashed down on the gas pedal, causing the diesel engine to race from idle. Over the roar of the engine I heard shouting.

Cops were screaming at the shooter I think. I couldn't make it out before I heard another shot followed by a hail of gunfire. It was over as quickly as it started, and all I could hear was the thundering whine of the engine.

I backed my foot off the gas. The sound of Greek Town nightlife had been replaced with screams, some crying.

Radio chatter, too. Police were talking.

I started to sit up, Hunter rising with me at the same time as we looked around wide-eyed.

"What the fuck… holy shit, Badger." He gestured at the gaping holes in the windshield. Turning back, he fingered the bullet hole in the wall segment directly behind where his head had been. "That almost took my fucking head off. Assholes!"

"Hunter." I swatted his shoulder to get his attention.

Through the cracks in the windshield I could see one of the DPD officers carrying someone draped in his arms. He was double timing it toward us and yelling for help. The seemingly lifeless body he carried looked female. Pretty young. The gown draping her frame said she was going to, or coming from, some formal event. Long tendrils of pearlescent white fabric were trailing behind, reflecting the reds and blues of the flashing light bars. The blood soaking through her gown glistened with each flicker of the squad car's strobes.

She looked pale enough to be dead twice over.

She looked a lot like Sarah.

"Time to go to work."

*****

5

Pupils are fixed and dilated. One gunshot wound to the chest... that's it? There's too much blood for just that one... maybe...

The officer already had a mask on the young woman's face, pushing oxygen into her with a steady rhythm. She was alive, but she wasn't going to stay that way for long. The bullet that hit her in the right breast created a sucking chest wound. Every breath was working to collapse that lung.

She looked so much like her... and then there were the gunshot wounds.

Focus. Focus and don't fuck this one up.

Hunter was barking over the radio for an ALS backup and additional units on scene as I trimmed the length of the blood-soaked gown open with my trauma sheers. Blood was pouring from an ugly hole in her right thigh, pooling on the cot beneath her.

Fucking Déjà vu.

"Hunter, get her airway, I've got the chest wound." I tugged the officer back and took the bag valve mask from his hands, making eye contact with him as I pushed a pile of gauze into his grip. "Put pressure on that leg and hold it."

Hunter already had the scope in and was sliding the tube into place. He's never missed an intubation on the first try, and he kept his streak tonight. I passed him the bag valve and he snatched the mask away, removing it to attach the bag directly to the tube.

All the chaos was forgotten in that moment. The gunshots, the ambulance taking fire, the dead kid in the street who went up against the officers and lost.

Didn't matter.

100% of me was in this moment.

Especially this moment.

After twelve years as a medic, it becomes like muscle memory. You start to work on autopilot.

I don't remember going through the motions but it seemed like just seconds and I had the chest seal in place. The flutter valve stopped any more air from being pulled into the chest cavity through the wound, while letting the air escape as Hunter continued to rhythmically squeeze the bag and fill her lungs with oxygen.

One quick cinch of a tourniquet and the pace of blood pulsing from her thigh slowed. My eyes went to the windows of the ambulance, scanning in every direction in hopes of seeing another crew.

"She's done if we don't go. We can't wait much longer for another rig." I rolled open my IV kit on the patient's naked abdomen, pulling a large bore catheter. My teeth clenched, sweat dripped off the tip of my nose as I struggled to get a line.

Her pulse was thready, and her veins were collapsing.

She was crashing, too.

Fuck, me. Not again.

The blood flashed into the catheter and I secured the line as Hunter continued to bag her

"We're going." I stood and nudged the cop toward the back. "Out unless you're ridin' along. Let's go."

The officer and I hopped from the back of the rig and I spun to shut the doors. As I bolted for the driver's seat the cop shouted after me, "What about the other one?"

I didn't bother looking back. "Other crew will be here in a minute."

"You can't leave, yet! Let the other ambulance take your patient." The cop reached a hand out and grabbed me around my bicep.

I spun in place, jerking my arm free from his grip.

"Write me a fucking ticket, I'll be at Receiving."

Stupid fuck.

Diving into the driver's seat I immediately flipped the row of switches across the console. My flashers and light bar bathed the street in a blinding dance of red and white strobes. I tapped the horn to alternate the tones that came screaming from the siren and gunned it.

My view was shit because of the fractured windshield, but I didn't let it slow me. I pulled the mic from the console as I weaved between the squad cars parked in the street.

"582." I released the mic and continued pushing through downtown traffic, waiting for the response from dispatch.

Sherry's voice came back over the radio with a crackle. "Go ahead, 582." I liked Sherry. She was a good dispatcher. Smart girl. Great tits. Not on my popular list tonight for posting us here though.

"Show us en route, priority one traffic to Detroit Receiving."

"Copy 582. Contact dispatch when you're clear."

8

I threw the mic into the passenger seat. "I hate this fucking car."

*****

All said and done, it's a normal occurrence. It's not every day that you're already sitting on scene when a bystander takes a few rounds from a handgun.

Still, it's routine shit. Less than 15 minutes of hell and chaos, and she's delivered to ER staff. She'll probably live if there are no complications, and only because we were already sitting there.

Otherwise she would have been one more body for the medical examiner.

My thoughts kept going to her face.

I stood at the front of the ambulance, gazing at the half-fractured windshield full of holes. That was a close call as well. A few feet to the right and it would have punched my ticket. If Hunter hadn't dropped, he'd be gone for sure. I took a drag from the cigarette and exhaled slowly, flicking the butt to the ground of the ER bay and smashing it out with my boot.

"Hey." Hunter had slid up into the cab through the pass through and had his face pressed into one the large holes in the windshield.

He looked like Nicholson grinning through the door in The Shining.

"Bitchin about my energy drinks while you suck on those things? Get back here and help me clean this shit up."

I walked quietly to the back of the rig, the open rear doors bathing the ER bay with the glow of the interior lights in the patient compartment. The cot sat parked against the truck and was covered in blood.

The floor had its fair share of bloody boot prints.

Bandages, wrappers, dirt – it seemed like more and more calls were turning into messes like this.

Less than fifteen minutes to save a life but twice that to clean up the mess.

Sometimes more when shit gets messy like this.

Fucking downtown car.

The newbies never expect this shit. Working an advanced life support rig is like a fairytale for them. The new medics in their early twenties, gung-ho to save a life, think that ALS crews are out here magically healing people before they get to the hospital.

They want to be heroes.

It takes calls like this, or worse, to shake their world and bring them back to reality.

Put them on a call where people start dying around them and they'll either wake up or wash out. A select few turn into 'paragods' – know-it-all trauma troopers riding the adrenaline rush from one 911 to the next.

Hunter started out like that.

I'll never forget the day he climbed into my truck as a fresh medic six years ago. The first question out of his mouth was about the worst call I had ever been on. Just hours later he was driving on a priority one and he bellowed a Tarzan yell over our truck's PA while running lights and sirens through an intersection.

He was a pure-blooded trauma trooper until he got his wakeup call.

Wouldn't trade him for anything now though.

"You gonna start cleaning that cot, or you wanna just stare at me like you're hoping I pull out my gigglestick?"

"I can't help it. You're such a pretty little bitch." I smirked and caught the roll of towels he threw at me.

"Shiiiiiiit. We both know I'm the top in this relationship."

"Forever and ever, babe." I kissed the air loudly in his direction and sprayed the stretcher down with disinfectant, setting to work on the cot mattress.

We weren't going to talk about what went down.

That's not how we do it.

We cope through twisted humor and we talk a lot of shit. We'll talk about it on another shift. Maybe a few days from now. Until then, the only time it will get brought up is when another crew asks. But then we'll brag about it. Hunter will embellish the gunshots and likely talk about his matrix-esque moves as the bullets sailed by his head.

And someone will inevitably ask, because across the forty-plus active crews running 911 backup around Metro Detroit at any given time, our truck was always the shit magnet.

Didn't matter where they stuck us, but it seemed to get worse if I was driving.

Hunter broke the silence.

"She looked like Sarah." I immediately stopped wiping and just stood there motionless. That son of a bitch was gonna talk about it.

"Are you kidding me right now?"

"I'm just saying, I'm surprised you didn't notice." He shrugged, which was about as close as you would ever get to anything resembling an apology. It was more an acknowledgement that he said something shitty.

"I noticed." I didn't look at him. I sprayed again and started scrubbing down the plastic padding of the Stryker cot with new-found aggression.

"Was kind of weird, though… right?" He moved to stand in the open doors of the patient compartment, one arm gripping the bar across the ceiling of the rig as he hung against the edge, looking down at me. "Same injuries, looked like her, same place."

I looked up at him and snapped back, "Yeah, I fucking noticed, ok? I don't want to talk about it and you should know that."

He shrugged again. "Maybe you should."

I threw the paper towel down on the cot and turned up to face him.

"Maybe you should eat my ass with a spoon." I glared at him.

Hunter was crossing a line that hadn't been edged against in the entirety of our run as partners. He hopped down from the truck without a word and squared off with me. His chest bumped mine, his head craning up almost comically given his small stature against my height. Our eyes darted back and forth at each other in silence.

He produced a small plastic package, waving the disposable cutlery between our faces.

"I have a spork."

"Jesus Christ." I laughed and shoved him off. Shaking my head, I went back to wiping down the cot – I wasn't really paying attention to cleaning it. It was more to keep my hands busy as my mind went in a thousand directions over the call and thoughts of her. My smile left me and I looked to Hunter. "Don't bring her up again. Not yet."

"Have you talked to Holly la-"

"Dude." I cut him off and looked upward, sighing.

"10-4. Whenever you're ready, boo. I got you."

Chapter 2 – Holding Fire

"Why do you make me come here, Badger?" Hunter stared down into his coffee cup, grimacing as he skimmed the top of the black drink with his spoon. "There's oil floating on my coffee."

"Actually, that's coffee floating on your oil." Cindy had perfect timing with her quips, always appearing out of nowhere to riff on Hunter and keep our cups full. She winked at me coyly, putting a fist to her hip and leaning into me. I could smell the White Diamonds old lady perfume she used to mask the scent of the deep fryer.

It didn't help, but it had long been her signature scent. The kind of pungent, unpleasant-yet-welcoming aroma you start to look forward to.

Like grandma's house, or puppy breath.

"Hey Bobbie, how are you babe?"

"I'm good, beautiful. Just coffee this morning." I gave her a warm and genuine smile. I loved Cindy like family. She was all of sixty years old and had been working this downtown Coney Island as long as I've been coming here – better part of a decade. Her face, hair, and body looked like she'd run it through the ringer, but her makeup and collection of ridiculous wigs said that she wasn't done living yet.

"Oh horseshit." She slapped my shoulder. "You're having an omelet. And so are you, boy." She snatched the menu out of Logan's hand.

"I can't say no to you, mama."

"I can." Hunter tried to stop her. "I don't want an omelet. Cindy... Cindy seriously!" He spun in his booth calling after her as she popped a middle finger over her shoulder at him. I let myself laugh good at that, it felt good feeling something normal.

"That's why I make you come here." I pointed after her as Hunter turned back, actually sulking a bit. "Because that's funny shit and... oh my God, are you pouting right now?"

"You wouldn't think it was funny if she gave you shit all the time. I swear I think she hates me." He shot a look over his shoulder before mumbling, "Her stank ass smells like the Great Depression."

"I don't hate you, Logan." Cindy slid up next to him with all the stealth and agility of a wild cat stalking its prey.

He practically hit orbit, jumping so high his knees shook the table and bounced our drinks. "Jesus CHRIST, where the fuck did you come from?"

"Mama's always nearby for her boys." She topped the coffee for us and mopped up the coffee Hunter had spilled. "And if you don't behave, I'm gonna wipe some of that stank on your eggs."

15

My head rocked back in laughter as Hunter shuddered in dramatic disgust. If there were any other patrons in the Coney Island aside from the half-dead drunks stumbling in from the bars, someone might be offended at the banter. We were never quiet about it. Not in the years we've been coming here. When a night car ends, we close it out right here in this booth.

Same shitty coffee. Same banter.

I sat in silence for a minute, still smirking as I stared at my coffee. I could see Hunter staring at me. He wanted to say something.

"Where did we leave off at?" There it is. He couldn't leave well enough alone. I let my head roll slowly and gave him a sideways stare.

"The thing with the states. That stupid game you started the last time we were here. Where'd we leave off?"

"Oh." I felt like a dick. I was still on edge about him bringing up Sarah, I thought he was gonna push the subject again. "Wisconsin. You did Wisconsin."

"Ok." He sits up and rubs his hands together. "I got one you can't figure out."

"Hit me with it."

Hunter grinned like a villain revealing his master plan. He was overly excited for this thing I had come up with the last time we worked this car. If the US were a high school, what kind of kid would each state be? Just some bullshit to pass the time. He was surprisingly creative, and it generated some good laughs, but he hadn't been able to stump me yet.

"Florida!" He slapped the table.

16

"Oh hell, that's easy." I straightened and lifted my chin, letting my eyes wander a moment to let him feel like he had me.

"Easy huh?"

"Remember when all the kids at the lunch table would dump their leftovers onto a single plate – spaghetti, milk, ten salt packets, pudding, ketchup, tuna…"

"Yeah…"

"Florida is the kid who would eat that for 43 cents."

"Shit…that was a good one. OK, do me." He waved both hands. "Gimme the hardest one you've got."

"O-" he cut me off, sticking his finger in my face.

"And don't fucking say Ohio!"

"I just thought it would be easy since you're from Monroe. That's practically Ohio." Tongue planted firmly in cheek, Hunter was a stone-cold Michigan fan. He'd sooner set fire to his body than have anything to do with Ohio.

He once turned down a threesome with a couple of curvy cougars at a bar just because they were from Toledo – at least that's how he tells it. Anyone who knew Hunter knew that was bullshit.

He'd put his dick just about anywhere, and he has.

"I swear to God, I'll crawl across this table and tea bag you with this swamp sack that's been brewing all shift."

"Alright, alright. Michigan then."

"Shit! That's not even hard. Michigan would be the girl who says she only dates country boys but low-key fucks black dudes."

17

Hunter spit that response out so fast it was like he'd been hanging on to it since birth. Cindy strolled over, setting our plates down with all the care of a grandmother serving her favorite grandkids. The steam rolled up and hit me with the scent of a cheese-stuffed farmer's omelet, grease, and Cindy's white diamonds. Familiar perfection.

"What's wrong with fucking black dudes?" Cindy smiled and leaned down, lowering her voice. "They're the only ones who keep my fuck hole satisfied." She gave a gentle pat to Hunter's shoulder and walked away. "Enjoy, Logan."

I could actually see a touch of pale green start to show in his face. He stared at his plate for a moment before pushing it away slowly. I wanted to laugh. I wanted to feel anything other than what I felt when I glanced over and saw a waitress walk by that looked just like her.

Sarah.

I scowled and looked again. It obviously wasn't her. It couldn't have been her.

It wasn't – not even close. Not even the same color hair.

My insides suddenly felt hollow. Hot, but empty. Saliva began to well up in my mouth and my stomach turned. I sat with eyes closed fighting the urge to vomit. Or scream. I'm not sure which it was.

"You ok, Bobbie?" He went with the first name rather than calling me by my last, like we always do. Like all crews do. He was genuinely concerned. I guess I wasn't hiding it well.

"I'm gonna go," I said flatly, sliding from the booth. "We're back on at 9am. I need sleep." I tossed a twenty onto the table, more than enough to cover the meal and a generous tip. Not that I was worried Cindy would be offended at skipping the food.

She'd be more upset I didn't say goodbye. I left without another word, punching through the doors of the Coney Island into the crisp dawn air.

*****

I paused on the city sidewalk next to my minivan and hung my head for a minute. I was shaky and could feel my heart pounding hard in my chest. Placing a hand on the side door, I leaned and felt my legs try to buckle under me.

She had been gone for nearly a year. I had only just recently stopped replaying things in my head again and again. Then this goddamned call tonight.

Detroit was starting to wake around me, and the empty city blocks would soon be filled with traffic mingling with pedestrians. But it was still quiet for now, and cold. It always felt colder downtown in the morning. The buildings blocked the sun's rays, and the wind was pulling chill air from the Detroit river.

I exhaled slowly and stood straight again, testing my legs.

I was such a goddamn failure. Sarah was dead, and it was my fault. It was always my fault, and I'm a piece of shit forever thinking it was OK to put it in the back of my mind. To try to forget. Why should I be able to forget and lock that away?

I shuddered and felt a new wave of nausea hit me. My vision blurred suddenly, briefly, before darkness started to close in around the edge of my sight – like being yanked back into a dark tunnel. I shook my head and gripped the side of the van to steady myself.

A car passed by, but there was no sound. Just a persistent ringing deep in my head. I reeled again and staggered a bit, catching myself on the side mirror. It felt like gravity suddenly shifted, or I had forgotten how to balance myself. My body seemed to be fighting my attempts to balance.

Easy, Bobbie. Steady. Slow, deep breathing. Slow exhale.

Slow inhale.

You murdering, son of a bitch.

Slow exhale.

You goddamn coward.

Slow inhale.

You killed her.

Slow exhale.

The angry words persisted, but I pushed them back down.

Just like always.

Slow, steady breathing.

In and out.

I kept my eyes closed to ward off the nausea, continuing the controlled breathing. I felt gravity right itself again, slowly. My heart began to slow again and I reached a trembling hand to my face, wiping it across my forehead.

I was drenched in sweat.

Pushing off from the van slowly, I tested my legs once again as my hands began to pat my pockets down out of habit.

"What the fuck…" I muttered under my breath.

I pulled the cigarette pack from the breast pocket of my uniform. My hands continued to shake as I held the zippo, flicking it repeatedly to spark a flame. The wind was playing hell with me, pushing hard through the city street between the tall buildings.

A SMART bus rocketed past, adding to the gust. I slid in closer to the van, tucking myself against the window and cupping my hands to get a flame. I took the first pull and closed my eyes, expecting the nicotine to instantly calm my nerves. Of course, it didn't.

I exhaled and opened my eyes to see last night's patient, or was it Sarah, poised directly behind me in the reflective tint of the van's window.

"FUCK!" Hunter and I screamed practically in unison as I spun on him and he jumped away from me.

"You scared the shit out of me, Hunter."

"Scared YOU? I think my dick just inverted. What the hell's the matter with you?! You been standing here staring at your van like a statue, man. Are you OK, Bobbie?"

I didn't have words to describe the volumes of terror I was feeling in that moment. I just shook my head and avoided eye contact, staring toward the ground. No way did I want to look up at him and see her. I shook my head hard again, tossed the cigarette, and bolted around the van to get behind the wheel.

"Bobbie!" Hunter had his hands up, staring through the passenger window at me. I started the engine.

"Where are you goin? Talk to me." He wrapped hard on the window with his knuckles and jiggled the handle on the passenger door. I yanked the shifter into drive and drove the gas to the floor. The tires chirped loudly as I rocketed away from the curb, leaving Hunter to shrink in the rearview of my Grand Caravan.

*****

After twelve years of driving the same routes home, I don't notice or pay attention to much. I can't count the number of nights I got home and couldn't recall a single part of the drive. Like I had slept through it, or teleported somehow.

That wasn't the case this morning. Everything was a distraction hitting me with sensory overload. My nerves settled some, but it was still an epic feat to stay focused.

Every other car on I-75 seemed like an impassable barrier.

Every overpass was a compelling opportunity to run my van head first at 80mph into the supports and just end it.

22

There was a constant, horrific feeling that something, or someone, was in the seat behind me – ready to end me. I must have checked the mirror a thousand times while I drove.

I couldn't get home fast enough, but as soon as I hit my street I felt compelled to keep driving. There was a Wayne County Sheriff parked in front of my house.

Holly.

Hunter probably called her.

I stepped inside and threw my keys onto the buffet next to the stairs. Straight down the hall I could see Holly, sitting at the table in the dining room. Her eyes were fixed on her smartphone, fingers dancing around on the screen. She was laid back relaxed in the chair, one leg crossed over the other with the phone in her lap.

I sniffled and leaned against the buffet, unzipping and kicking off my tactical boots as I released half the buttons down my uniform shirt.

Holly sniffled.

It wasn't necessarily intentional – at least not consciously. It was just our thing; more of a habit. Somewhere over the years, we started doing that when we would see each other. A 'what's up?' without words. Despite not seeing each other for months after she left, it was like nothing changed. Old habits die hard.

Everything was different though. Everything had changed.

I wanted to go the opposite direction, right back out the door. I didn't have it in me to face her. But at the same time, every fiber of my being needed to smell her hair and feel her embrace. My eyes traced the curves of her body that no duty belt and bullet proof vest could hide.

Holly had the skill, equipment, and the heart to hunt down and eviscerate what was haunting me, and I needed her desperately for that.

I also hated her right now, surprisingly. There was more lingering anger than I had thought.

Despite padded socks, my feet still fell with hollow thuds as I made my way down the hall. Compliments of the well-aged hardwood floors and crawl space of the old Victorian home. Not that I was trying for stealth. Holly wasn't a woman you try to sneak up on – not when she had 15 years of close-combat and weapons training, with a Springfield XD holstered on her well-rounded waistline.

With a slow inhale and audible sigh, I stopped in the entry to the kitchen and dining area and leaned against the frame.

"What are you doing, Holly?" My arms crossed over my chest as I scowled.

"Playing Candy Crush." She didn't look at me. Instead, her fingers continued to play across the screen on her phone.

"I… know. I can see that." My irritation grew and I was already at the edge. "What are you doing in my house?"

"Playing Candy Crush." She finally looked at me as she spoke, and I felt the strength go out of me. The blonde curls that framed her face jostled slightly as her soft, almond shaped blue eyes locked with mine. Sarah looked so much like her mother. I tasted ash in my mouth. The moisture left my tongue, and I struggled to swallow. "And it's our house, Bobbie."

She tossed the phone on the table and stood up, stepping toward me. She was an impressive woman, even at just 5'4". There weren't too many people that could intimidate me, but Holly always had enough swagger in her posture that I knew she could throttle me if she wanted to.

The fact that she was a veteran with the Sheriff's department also helps.

That didn't matter right now, because I was fucking pissed.

"My house. You left, remember?" I thumbed over my shoulder. "You cut and run."

"Don't you dare put that on me, Bobbie." She stepped in closer and jabbed her finger in my chest. The volume in her voice started to climb immediately. "You shut down on me, what choice did I – You know what…" She covered her face with one hand and shook her head. "I… I don't want to do this. I'm sorry. I didn't come here to fight with you. I needed to see you."

"You wanted to see me, or did Hunter call you?"

"Both." She put her hands on my chest. "Hunter told me about the call. I came to check on you."

I could smell her now as she moved in close.

25

It was strange to feel absolute anger with someone, but have your heart ache over yearning. As tense as I was, with my teeth mashed tightly together, the instant her fingers touched me through the fabric of my shirt I thought I was going to lose the last bit of control I had.

Everything inside me twisted in a confused mass of sorrow, anger, joy, love, and lust.

Holly just looked at me as I stood in silence. I felt so weak and dizzy, like even the softest touch from her would send me reeling to the floor. But her touch was comforting; made me feel safer. I could spend an eternity taking in the scent of lavender shea butter that always hung around her.

Her hand rose to touch my cheek, running over the short hairs of my beard. I had no more strength to contain it. My lip quivered and I felt my chest quake as my head fell forward.

"I killed our baby." The words came out in a silent whisper, draped in tears that had been held in for far too long. I hadn't seen Holly in months, and seeing her now brought it all back in a torrent that I simply couldn't hold back anymore.

My arms fell as I turned to lay my back against the wall. Holly embraced my face with her soft hands, pulling my eyes level with hers. Her features had softened, or it may have been the blur as I looked to her through watery eyes.

"No. Bobbie, no," she said sternly, though the look on her face was abject sincerity. "No, you did not. You did everything you thought you could do, Bobbie."

She used her thumbs to wipe the tears from my face as I stood, quaking in front of her.

"Bobbie, baby, I don't blame you. I never blamed you. I never once thought it was on you. Don't put that on yourself."

I inhaled, breathing out slowly to try and regain control of my emotions. It was a monumental task given my exhaustion. Anger welled again.

I scoffed a bit, wiping at my eyes.

"If that's how you feel, then why did you leave?"

Her lips pursed and I watched her shoulders settle. Her hands slid back to my chest. "You shut me out, Bobbie! You stopped talking. You stopped eating with me. You were taking back to back 24 hour shifts and avoiding home."

"You were avoiding me."

Holly's eyes started to water and her voice cracked. "You stopped touching me. We lost Sarah… and then I was losing you. I panicked. Bobbie, I'm sorry."

Tell her you love her.

I put my hands on top of hers, holding them to my chest. "You left me when I needed you most, Holly." I was compelled to push her away from me, but I also wanted to pull her in close to me and envelop her in my arms. I felt like I was at war with myself.

Tell. Her. You. Love. Her.

"Bobbie... just because I left, doesn't mean I stopped loving you." Holly looked up to me again, her eyes were searching mine for some sign. I wanted to tell her that it was alright. That I loved her, fiercely, with all I had. Her admission felt like a cleansing, and it lifted a terrible weight – but not all of it. I still felt anger, wrapped in sorrow.

You're a goddamn fool.

I wanted to embrace her, and could see that she longed for it as much as me. It's the biggest cowardice of a man to awaken the love of a woman without the intention of loving her back.

"I didn't know what to do without you, Holly. Every day was hell." I clasped her hands and pulled them together, holding them tightly to my chest.

A small laugh escaped her, more out of relief I think. She sniffled and sighed, gripped my hands tightly and smiled up at me.

I sniffled back.

Her fingers wiggled in my hands, the tips of her nails finding the exposed flesh of my chest. Holly's eyes moved to where she had touched me and she slid her hands forward slowly from my grip, pressing her palms softly into my pecs. She looked back up to me as I felt her fingers gently squeeze my chest.

Plain as day, the small light she had for me in her eyes burst into a glowing flame with all the subtlety of a napalm enema.

28

I was fighting with myself again, suddenly aware of the heat growing between us. Aware of the hushed, fragile silence in our home save for her breath. Her chest heaved and she inhaled, leaning up and into me. She was offering me her lips.

God, did I want her, but she wasn't going to get anything like that from me.

Not that easily.

"I have to go back to the station soon." I looked down and swallowed hard, trying to push the craving for her thick hips back down deep from where it had surfaced.

Her head cocked to the side as our gaze met, and her eyes narrowed – hardening her face a little as she pursed her lips. Her right hand took mine, squeezing softly again before she wrenched my wrist, twisting my left arm and turning it behind me. The maneuver forced me to pivot and she shoved her elbow into my back. I could smell the plaster in the wall as my forehead bounced against it.

That might do it though…

She kicked my legs apart, effortlessly immobilizing me against the wall as I groaned, using my free hand to keep her from pressing me through the wallboards.

"You're not going to work today, Bobbie," she hissed quietly into my ear. "You don't feel well." While keeping my wrist wrenched at a wicked angle behind my back, she ran her other hand under and between my legs.

We both discovered that I was hard.

My eyes closed as I felt her fingers. It had been so long.

"Do you have a permit for this?"

I exhaled and let out a light laugh. Before I could answer I felt her fingers clamp down on my cock through my trauma pants. Her other hand tugged my wrist, twisting my arm higher. Pain exploded up my arm. Beautiful, sweet pain. My eyes watered and I clenched my teeth.

"Is something funny? I asked you a question!" She dug her nails through the fabric, pinching deep. "Do you have a permit for this weapon, son?"

"No ma'am," I whispered sharply between panting and gasping through the pain, but I didn't want it to stop. Nothing else existed in that moment but Holly and I, and it was like nothing had changed. I tried to crane my neck to look back and down at her while she groped and squeezed. She stood up quickly, mashing an elbow into the back of my head.

I rocked forward, my mouth smacking against the wall.

I tasted blood and my ears rang.

"Don't you dare eye-fuck me."

I felt her foot come down hard on the back of my knee, dropping me. I could smell the cool earth of the crawlspace through the floor. I felt every grain of dirt on the wood. I couldn't see her but I could hear the blood pounding in her veins.

My senses seemed to be on overload.

"Do you want to eye-fuck me?"

"No ma'am," I lay dead still, panting. My eyes were fixed on the baseboards. They were dusty from months of neglect. Without Holly here, everything had been neglected.

But she was here now.

"Do you want to fuck me?"

Fuck that bitch

I didn't answer.

She placed her foot on the side of my neck and jaw and began to press down.

"I asked you a question, asshole." The pressure increased on my neck and I groaned through the pain.

Shove that cock right down her fucking throat

"Yes ma'am," I croaked out quietly.

"Get on your knees."

I crawled up slowly, jolts of pain still springing from my wrist and elbow, my jaw throbbing. Flecks of dirt were stuck to my cheek. I wanted more of it. I kneeled before her, my eyes staring directly at her duty belt. I didn't dare look up at her.

Or did I?

My eyes went up, and I instantly felt the sharp strike of an open hand slap. My already throbbing jaw exploded in pain and my ears rang. The stinging in my cheek was bliss. I smiled a little as I tipped sideways from the hit, but hid that wry grin from her sight.

Back to my knees. It's what she wanted. My eyes were back to her duty belt.

Her hands moved expertly, unfastening it while I watched. She lifted it in front of me and then held it to the side, letting it drop with a heavy thud. Holly's hands closed around my head, and she pulled me close, pressing my face to her body. I could smell her again. The lavender shea butter mixed with her body's own sweet scent.

I could feel the heat of her pussy as she ground her hips into my face.

I exhaled fully in my desire, adding to the heat. She pulled upward on my head and I complied, quickly getting to my feet – though shaky and reeling. That was when I saw her.

Not with anger, or frustration, or sorrow. I saw my Holly through the spectacles of absolute infatuation and love.

By the way she looked at me, with her chest heaving, face glowing with a silky layer of sweat and flushed, she was seeing me that way as well.

Time hung. Everything was silent again as we stared. I'm not sure who moved first but we were suddenly in one another's arm in a crushing embrace. Our mouths met angrily, devouring one another noisily. There was no rhythm.

She bit my lip.

Our tongues danced.

We bounced from one wall to the frame of the kitchen door. We bit at each other more.

Her hands fumbled with my belt as I quickly tugged at the buttons of her shirt, refusing to unlock our mouths from one another. When the last of her shirt was tugged free she flailed, tearing it from her body.

She removed the bulletproof vest with the same ferocity, throwing it across the kitchen. I watched her practically shred the sport bra, and I never wanted her more. She grinned at me, panting, with her beautiful bare breasts heaving.

They were better than I remembered, and it made me ache for her. She had perfect breasts – not too large, just about a handful but they were full and perky. They went well with the extra hips and ass she sported, only outdone by the thick, dark nipples that always stole my attention.

Holly stepped to me, passing through a hard ray of morning light that punched through the kitchen. It lit her face like a goddamn angel, but there was absolutely zero angelic innocence inside her right now.

She kissed me softly this time and my hands cupped her breasts, squeezing hard. I missed her flesh, and I'd have reached deep inside her if I could. My hands conveyed what words could not, rolling her nipples between my fingers, alternating between tugging gently and firmly.

Her lips parted in a soft moan as she broke our kiss.

"I need you inside me." Holly trembled against me, and I could feel her hot breath.

With all the gentleness she had showed me, I spun her away, pushing her toward the table. Unclasping her pants, she started to slide them down as if to take them off. I grabbed her hand to stop her just as the waistline dropped below the voluptuous curves of her ass, revealing her black thong.

Grabbing her by the back of the neck I bent her over, pressing her into the table. She was gasping and I stood, staring. She writhed under my grip, just a little. Her back twisted and her hips came up.

She tried to move back into me, searching for me. One of her hands pressed to the table, the other came back, searching along the crotch of my pants. I stepped out of her reach and she whimpered.

Fuck her.

Still bent, her hips swayed and moved, quietly begging for me. I slid my pants down with no grace, like a teenager stumbling toward his first conquest. Stepping back to her I felt like I was already near climax. Her hand reached for me again, and her fingers gently caressed the tip when she found it – only briefly. As soon as she felt it, she breathed heavily and wrapped her hand around it, tugging hard and moaning.

Pulling her thong to the side, I slid my fingers down her ass and deep between her legs. Her pussy was hot and swollen, nearly dripping and slick as I cupped her sweet flesh and kneaded it with my fingers.

Her hips bucked and she groaned.

Fuck. Her.

I stole myself from her grip and her ass rose again. She spread her legs as much as she could with her slacks only partially down. I moved into her in one motion, burying my cock to its base in a slow, steady drive, each hand settling to grip a pound of her curvy hips.

It was almost overwhelming to feel how tight she was.

She sucked air, gasping and letting out a cry, gripping the table to push back against me. I thrust again, dragging her back into me by her hips. Her skin was shiny, damp with sweat, glistening in the morning light that poured through the windows.

With every thrust, ripples danced along her ample ass.

We settled into a rapid, rough rhythm. She was throwing herself back into me, and I pushed into her with all I had. My hand went to her hair, grabbing up her golden curls and dragging her head up and back.

"Is this what you needed, ma'am?" I whispered into her ear as I squat slightly and continued to pound deep inside her dripping pussy. With every thrust I tried to go deeper, and with every thrust I could feel her muscles clamping down on me, like she didn't want to let me out once I was inside her.

My free hand cradled her breast, pulling at her nipple.

"Oh, fuck me, Bobbie. Yes!"

I felt her muscles stiffen as she gasped, her shoulders convulsing while pushing back hard, trying to swallow every inch of me with her hungry lust.

Light bursts filled my eyes as I felt myself begin to peak. I couldn't, in that moment, describe what I was feeling for her.

There are things we feel for certain people, and only they make us feel those things.

This was one of those. More than a climax.

Deeper than love.

Indescribable.

It drained me.

Pushing her back to the table I grabbed her by her hips and pumped faster. She was dragging her nails on the table, moaning loudly as I came.

My cock throbbed as I pressed deep and I tossed my head back, a slow yell beginning to escape, growing into a thunderous roar – taking with it the last of my ability to stay on my feet.

Our screams mingled as we came together, our movement slowing suddenly as my legs quaked.

There was suddenly not enough oxygen in the room for us. Like fish out of water we were gasping desperately and gulping for air.

We said nothing.

We stayed there, collapsed together atop the table.

Chest to back.

Wind chimes rang softly, briefly outside the dining room window next to us. Holly had hung them just before she left.

All else had been forgotten. For now.

*****

Half propped up on pillows, I glanced to her as she stirred in bed.

Her lithe, yet curvaceous figure shifted as she slept. She was facing away from me, her side rising and falling in shallow, rhythmic breaths.

My eyes wandered down her body again, the milky skin a strong contrast to the dark bed cover she lay on. Her blonde curls fell around her as her hips shifted and slid a few inches across the silky fabric.

"You're so beautiful."

It didn't register. She was out cold.

I checked my phone again, staring at the time. Only minutes had passed since the last time I checked it.

Time wasn't hanging anymore, and my face fucking hurt.

And my jaw.

God, I love this woman, but she hits like a bullet train. So many laughable stories of getting pulled into transport calls for her scenes, usually because some bear thought he could get one over on this little lady.

She was a crazy bitch.

'Never stick your dick in crazy' they say.

They're missing out.

She purred quietly, almost inaudible and rolled, stretching a bit as she lay on her back. Her breasts slid into view. All natural, full, and still wonderfully pert despite laying on her back and coming up on 40.

I caught myself smiling. I had missed her so much.

But part of me was still so pissed. Forgiving her wasn't that easy.

But who the fuck am I to hold a grudge after what I did?

Or didn't do.

"Fuck me… fucking asshole." I rubbed a hand around my face, sniffling and sighing heavily.

I looked to her face, mouth open like a guppy. Sarah had gotten all of her features. Very few of mine. She looked just like her mother, and Holly loved that.

Liked to rub it in. Said it wasn't right for a lady to look like a mob enforcer.

'Mommy raised a princess, daddy raised a savage.' That's what Sarah used to say about us.

I checked my phone again. I needed to decide if I was calling out or going back in soon.

My head fell back against the headboard and I stared at the ceiling, naked. Reaching without looking, I pawed for the pack of cigarettes on the side table and sat up on the edge of the bed.

Holly hated that I smoked, and she would give me shit when she woke. I had quit years ago, but everything that happened with Sarah was just too much. I started smoking again. Not much, a few a shift. A pack lasted me a couple days. Maybe less if shit was thick.

"What the fuck happened this morning..." I mumbled and took a long drag, blowing the smoke down toward the floor, elbows resting on my knees.

I dug at my eye with a thumb, trying to remember the last time I had slept. Was it yesterday? I was exhausted, drained, but couldn't sleep. Couldn't nap. I could only sit here, my mind racing over last night's call.

I checked my phone again, looking at the time as a notification popped.

Hunter: "You up?"

I stared at the words, my thumb hovering over the onscreen keyboard. I clicked the screen off and tossed the phone behind me on the bed, flicking the ash on the floor before taking another long drag.

He was right.

The patient had looked just like Sarah, a bit older though. That girl looked the part of someone celebrating turning twenty-one downtown.

Not that it was any kind of significant milestone around here. Not really.

I don't think there's a local alive who hasn't crossed the Ambassador Bridge into Canada to enjoy the minimum drinking age of 19. That wouldn't stop the flow of shots in the city when they hit twenty-one, though.

Sarah was younger, was still a baby in my eyes. She was downtown with friends after a homecoming dance.

My baby.

My eyes closed and I hit the cigarette again, exhaling slowly, hanging my head.

I see it all happening. All the time.

Over and over again. All the goddamn time.

Every time I'm alone with my thoughts, there she is. Reaching for me and crying.

It doesn't matter how long you've been in this shit. Everything can flip shit when the person on the ground is someone you know. When it's your sister, or a friend, or a coworker.

God forbid it's your little girl.

Hunter and I were on our way back to post at the casino after wrapping up a call to take in some girl who had lost herself down a k-hole and was fucking blitzed. Laying half-naked on the sidewalk, begging to be used... kidnapped... murdered.

Blue and black fishnet leggings. Matching little skintight dress that barely covered anything and left plenty hanging out.

Blonde hair with purple and blue streaks.

39

"Fuck."

I smirked. It's funny how memorable that call was, plain as day, because of what happened after.

I was driving when we got the call priority 1 back into Greek Town for a gunshot victim.

The cigarette was burning into the filter. I could feel the heat on my fingers. I punched it out in the ashtray.

I lit another.

Standard shit. 'Living the fucking dream.' I remember Hunter was throwing a goddamn tantrum the whole way back. Ranting about hoods, gangs, 'motherfucking' this and 'motherfucking' that.

I was laughing at him as I drove, weaving through traffic to get on scene.

We almost got blasted by an Escalade with spinners and illegal tint going through a red. Hunter screamed at them over the P.A, his angry shouts echoing briefly before being swallowed by the chirps and wails from the siren.

Deep inhale, slow exhale.

There was a hefty crowd and absolute chaos on scene. Phones were out and up in the air, trying to get video over and around the DPD who were struggling to get the mob to back the fuck off.

Cot, jump bag, all that shit.

Standard shit.

Hunter was shoving people, shouting to get out of the way. He put a boot to the ass of a few people. They finally cleared a fucking path.

Then the whole clusterfuck world stopped spinning. I went numb.

I wasn't breathing. I stopped. Hunter got jerked to a halt as I stood there, holding the other end of the cot, staring at her on the ground.

Sarah.

40

He looked at me, then to her, and dove to the ground with the bag.

I went to take a hit of the cigarette but the entire length of ash fell away.

Ugh.

Hunter yelled back to me but I couldn't hear him. I couldn't hear a goddamn thing. I could only see her laying on the sidewalk. Her white homecoming gown covered in blood.

There were a dozen other kids, hovering, crying nearby, dressed in gowns and baggy untailored suits that looked ridiculous on the underdeveloped frames of the boys.

I walked to her and got on my knees. Hunter was working furiously. I don't remember what he was doing. I was just staring into Sarah's eyes.

She was awake and crying.

Sarah shivered and looked at me, looked through me. Convulsing and gasping it seemed to take forever for her eyes to recognize me.

'...Daddy,' she said softly and reached for me with shaky hands covered in blood. She was so pale.

She was dying.

'Daddy...' she reached for me and I touched her hand. She started to say something when Hunter shoved a rebreather into my hand. I stared at it briefly. I didn't know what to do with it.

Hunter didn't hesitate when I only stared. He took it away and slid it over her face.

He continued working furiously on her leg.

I shivered in the bedroom and took a drag. The hairs stood on my arm and I felt a chill roll over me. My phone chirped, vibrating twice on the bed behind me. Hunter again, probably.

41

He tried so hard to save her.

Hunter was my miracle.

It wasn't good enough. None of it was.

I watched him expertly stop the heavy flow from a gunshot wound to her thigh. There was so much blood.

Hunter was yelling at me.

We had to go or she was done.

I started to come back, looking back to Sarah. Squeezing her hand.

"I got you, baby," I said aloud, Holly stirring behind me on the bed.

"I got you…"

I jumped in back. Hunter drove.

No, that's incorrect.

Hunter somehow swapped the ambulance's diesel engine out for jet propulsion, because that crazy asshole was flying.

I worked furiously on Sarah.

Her eyes were watching me, her head bouncing with each weave of the ambulance.

She wasn't moving.

She wasn't breathing.

It was the other gunshot wound. In through her flank.

Official report determined she died from cardiac arrest, secondary to respiratory arrest as a result of the sucking chest wound that collapsed her lung.

I could have saved her.

I should have saved her.

Such a stupid oversight.

I killed her.

42

She didn't even die in my arms, I didn't even get that much. She died on a cold stretcher, in the back of a loud angry box rocketing toward a hospital.

She died because of me.

You're such a fuck. FUCK.

"I'm sorry, baby." I trembled again. Had it been a year yet? Maybe less. I don't know. Holly had been gone for a couple months.

Murdering FUCK!

Holly stirred again behind me, and coughed sharply. I looked back to her, seeing the sun rays from the half-open blinds cutting a path through the smoky haze that hung in the room. I smashed out the last of the cigarette.

"Jesus Bobbie…" She coughed harder, grumbling.

"Sorry." I stood and cracked the window next to the bed, turning back to look at her.

"Go make some coffee for me?" She stretched slow like a cat, smiling at me playfully as she posed among the dark covers.

"Yeah. Coffee." I exhaled a soft, quiet sigh. "Sure."

*****

I had dug out the French press for her. She hated the single-serve cup machine that I got her at Christmas. Well, the coffee really. We both loved the machine until she tried a cup. After multiple brands of coffee, she gave up and went back to the French press.

It had sat unused, but I hadn't forgotten how to make it for her. Hopefully the coffee was still good. Beans were still in the freezer, freshly ground.

She was picky as hell when it came to coffee.

I stood nude in the kitchen, hands on my hips, staring at the French press while the coffee steeped.

The handle rattled and the front door opened. Peering around the kitchen entry to look down the hallway, I watched Hunter as he walked in. He didn't see me, didn't say anything, just slowly shut the door behind him. He looked to me as he started to make his way toward the kitchen.

"Hey man. I got your paper." He held it up and I nodded. "I text you to let you know I was coming, didn't you g-"

He came up short as he rounded the corner into the kitchen.

"Whoa. That's a penis." His eyes went straight to the ceiling and darted around.

His eyes fell to my face as I stared at him.

Then he looked back down to it, and back up to me before he about faced and sat at the table.

"Is that what you do at home between shifts? Soak your twig and berries in protein and miracle grow or something?" He tossed the paper on the table and looked at me again, shaking his head and making a disgusted face.

"It's just a penis. You have a penis." I dabbled in mild amusement. This was the normal shit between us on any given day, and normal felt good right now.

The banter was a good distraction.

44

"Penis is fine! I don't have a problem with penis. *I am OK with penis*." I poured a cup for Holly while he orchestrated his argument, animating his body as much as possible. He couldn't help it; his hyper-metabolic ass doesn't do well cooped up in the rig. Give him open space and he's like a hyperactive husky.

'Run. Run. Run? RUN.'

My mood was improving as I turned back. His eyes fell on my package again and he scoffed.

"We've all seen penises we weren't supposed to see." I smirked, shrugging slightly to mock Hunter's inability to apologize save for the dismissive gesture.

"Penis is fine," he said flatly. "That…" he pointed, "is not a penis. Do the Jamaicans know what you've done to their Olympic bobsled?"

"It is my house that you walked into. It's my penis' native land. His people roam free here."

Holly entered the kitchen, sauntering toward me. She took the cup from me with a little flourish and a curtsy, flaring her hips and ass back toward Hunter.

She was also naked.

"Thank you, sir." She winked at me with a wry smile. She hadn't called me 'sir' in a long time.

She turned back, giving Hunter a full-frontal shot as we kept our eyes locked on her. "Good morning, Hunter."

45

He watched her go by, his mouth hanging open, face flushed red, head slowly swiveling as she passed. Leaning hard in the chair, he craned his neck to get the long exposure. The wooden chair groaned as he tipped it. I was expecting the chair to break under the stress.

Or dump him on the floor.

I watched him mouth, quite expressively, the words 'OH. MY. GOD.'

"Hey. Cut it out."

He spun in the chair back toward me and recoiled, groaning loudly.

"DUDE… you're *hard*! It gets BIGGER?!" He looked back down the hall again, hoping to catch another glimpse of Holly. The look of tragic longing on his face told me that his tranquil view had ended. "I need to come over more often…"

"You wanna go fuck her?" I pointed toward the hallway.

His head snapped back at me so fast I struggled to keep a straight face.

"Uh… mother-fuck-yessir, I do."

"Too bad. She doesn't eat pussy." I walked toward the hallway, guessing at the time given Hunter's arrival. "Lemme get changed and we'll head in."

"Cool…" he hollered after me. "I'll just go hop in the back of the van so your… giant… dragon cock can ride shotgun."

Chapter 3 – Ride Along

Hunter was leaning against the rail of the big wooden porch, his back against a faux column supporting the covered porch. With arms crossed, his eyebrows went up as I came out. I was scowling hard, a V carved in the middle of my forehead by the scrunched muscles of my brow.

"Everything cool?"

"Fine." I let the screen swing shut behind me, the metal slamming loudly and echoing in the neighborhood. I slung the tactical bag over my shoulder containing my usual crop of shit to get me through a 24.

Cigarettes, Gameboy – the original one, protein bars, drink mix, fresh socks, backup charger, tablet, gum… and all the other comforts to make being stuck on a 24 just a bit more bearable.

The bag felt like it was filled with all the shit I was dragging around in my head. I was exhausted.

I just needed to get through this 24.

I made no plan to sleep on shift. That shit will guarantee back to back calls all day long. I'll just sleep hard when this shit show is over.

Marching down the porch, a little ragdoll stagger to my steps, I hit the release of the key fob, the side door rolling open. I was still scowling, standing there strapping my bag into the rear captain seat.

Hunter came up next to me, hands in his pockets, just staring at me.

He didn't stare long. Never does.

"So…"

I cut him off. I already knew where he was going. You could have heard Holly yelling at me at the end of the block.

"Yeah, she's pissed. She wanted, heh, *expected* me to call out." I shook my head and leaned against the van.

"She's just worried, bro. I mean, that call and all, with Sarah, you kinda went catatonic at the Coney. You scared the piss out of me, looked like you were going to jump me or something."

He shrugged again.

"I had to call her." He just stood there quietly a moment, waiting for me to acknowledge him. "I mean, I don't fuck you and I'm worried about you."

My hand rubbed at my forehead as I leaned against the van.

"I'm just tired, man."

"Then stay home. Be sick. Play with your wife's big, beautiful, amazing titties." He laughed, a little uncomfortably, trying to insert some levity. "Fuck, dude, I'd call out if I were you. But you know me. I go where you go, boo."

"Yeah, I appreciate that."

48

The front door of the house opened and Holly came out, swinging the screen hard and letting it bang against the wood siding. She was back in full uniform and came marching straight for me.

She still looked pissed.

"Ooooh shit, ok, I'm gonna get my bag." Hunter about-faced and took long strides toward his truck in the street as Holly came up short in front of me, staring at me with cold, hard eyes.

"How are you just gonna walk out like that?" She folded her arms across her chest. This Holly was decidedly not-sexy Holly right now. My eyebrows went up at her question.

"You really think that's the kind of question you can ask me?" My scowl found its way back as anger boiled up.

"Goddammit, Bobbie, you shouldn't be working. You need to stay home so we can finally talk. Why are you going in?"

"I already told you. We *just* went over this. *I told you why.* Is this what you want to do, stand here and fight in front of the neighbors?" I waved an arm. "I just want to fucking go to work and get this shift over with Holly."

Her frown deepened.

My heart felt heavy. Heavier than my bag.

Heavier than all the baggage I've ever carried.

"We'll talk after, okay? I just want to work, get some sleep, then I'll call you to come back over."

"Fine."

I stared at her and sighed, deflating a great deal as my shoulders fell. I extended my arms and stepped toward her.

49

Holly didn't move at first but, moving closer, her arms released from her chest and wrapped around me as she stepped in close. She squeezed me hard, burying her face in my chest. I found solace in the scent of her, my face turned into her loose curls.

We didn't say anything. Didn't have to. If you were standing nearby you could likely feel the tension gradually ease. Not completely, but enough. I held the embrace longer than usual, and she was making no effort to let go.

Our arms released their grip almost simultaneously, though slowly. Meeting her gaze I was relieved to see her face and eyes had softened.

"Call me. Please?" Her eyes were pleading as she placed a hand on my chest.

"I will."

"I love you, Bobbie."

"I know."

There's no easy explanation for why I couldn't say the words. The ball of emotions and turmoil I wrestled furiously was like a web of Christmas tree lights. There was no discernable start or end, just an unmanageable web of 'what the fuck'. The words just weren't getting past all that shit.

Of course, I loved her.

I loved Holly fiercely.

But I didn't deserve her, or her love.

Her eyes were steady gazing into mine.

"Bobbie, if my love could save you... you would live forever."

Tell her... you... love her.

"Holly…" I looked at her, and she nodded.

"Yup, I know. Be safe, baby." She looked down and walked away.

I caught her hand and stopped her, pulling her back toward me.

She didn't resist. My arms enveloped her again and I put my lips to hers. I couldn't bring myself to say the words.

I hoped to God she could feel it.

That maybe just a little of what I felt for her would find its way out through the mess and reach her.

She deserved to know.

Our lips barely touched as I kissed her. It was a soft kiss. Fragile. Symbolic.

The kiss she returned to me told me she understood. She increased the pressure – just a little. It was delicate, slow, deliberate. Her hand went to the back of my head.

It was the kind of kiss… I don't know. I can't remember another time it was like this. There's no comparison. Every other time we've communicated without words, it was passionate. Rough.

When we dated in school, seeing each other on break during college, the engagement, her deployment, her return from deployment and all the R&R in between. We weren't the soft, deliberate, sensual touch kind of couple.

The kind of soft, soul-swapping shit you'd see talked about in a romance novel didn't really come into play.

But I knew that she knew. That's what mattered to me. That was enough. She wanted me to be safe, to save me. But I couldn't have her out there trying to protect the county, distracted by me.

That would kill her.

We came apart and her hand touched my face, rubbing the short stubble of my chin. She smiled softly, and it made the air warmer around us.

"I'll see you." I let her go as she walked toward her car.

Hunter walked back up, whistling slowly, as Holly's patrol car pulled out of the drive.

"Looked like you were getting awful friendly there, Badger."

"Shut up and get in, we're gonna be late." I started to walk around to the driver's side when I heard her voice across the street. It was shrill, but delicate and sweet in a way.

"Bobbie! Oh, Bobbie, hi!" I turned and waved as my eyes scanned across the street. There she was standing up her driveway on the side of her house.

Lily Merriam. The sweetest woman you would have expected to stop walking the earth a decade ago. She and her husband were here when Holly and I bought this house almost 20 years ago.

Even then Lily was ancient.

Her husband, Everette, passed a few years back, and if it crippled her in any way she certainly didn't show it. Her grandson had moved in after Everette died - to help around the house with all the things Everette used to do. He was pretty spry for being like two hundred.

Lily was still a bundle of smiles.

Made it all the more annoying to see the grandson not giving her the assistance she needed.

"Good morning, Lily!" I made sure it was loud enough for her to hear. She didn't have hearing problems that I was aware of, but it was just one of those things with really…really old people. Loud and slow.

I forced a big smile and waved wide as I opened the door. She came shuffling down her driveway.

"Bobbie, Bobbie wait!"

I sighed and looked at Hunter sitting in the passenger seat. He put a finger gun to the side of his head and snapped his thumb down. His other hand gestured an explosion from the other side as he let his head fall backward.

"Just go, Hunter. I'll meet you at the station. She needs help with something. It'll be a little bit."

"I'm good, Bobbie." He stopped playing dead and sat up. "It's cool, Bae."

He leaned into the driver's side and whispered to me, "Don't show her your dick though, you'll give the poor old Q-tip a heart attack."

I looked to Lily, standing at the end of her drive wringing her hands together. She saw me make eye contact and waved me over frantically.

"No, go on ahead to the station. Get the truck ready. I don't want to get shit on for being late rolling to post." I shut the door and started to walk across the street as Hunter hopped out, shouldering his bag. I waved to him as I jogged. "I'll be right behind you."

*****

Lily was almost comically short at about 4'9" or so, made only sillier when I would stand next to her. She toddled to me with a slightly cocked head and a warm smile, wrapping her thin arms around my torso. She pressed the side of her cheek into my stomach and hugged me.

"Hi Lily, how are you?"

She backed up with small steps and pat me on the stomach before smoothing down my uniform shirt.

"OH. I'm fine." She turned and started to walk in quick, short steps up the slope of her driveway. She beckoned me to follow with a wave. I did, and had to greatly reduce my stride and pace to match hers. She wrapped an arm around mine to steady herself, which seemed to help her add a bit of speed to her pace.

We weren't going to hit plaid or ludicrous speed, but at least we'd make it to the house before the end of my shift.

"Was that Holly? I wanted to give her some things my daughter used to wear, she just doesn't want them anymore but refuses to get them out of the basement here." She smacked her lips and waved a hand. "I can't carry the boxes or I would just bring them to you, Bobbie."

"Yeah, Holly came by to talk." Lily knew a lot about what had happened. Just about all of it, actually.

When we lost Sarah, Lily brought us casseroles a plenty. There were many a night she insisted I come eat dinner with her after Holly left. Short of the crews at work, she was the only one I spoke with for the longest time.

Which led to me helping her around the house quite a bit. Fair trade for helping me keep my sanity and not letting me starve. The help was kind of a necessity anyhow. Her grandson had turned into a hefty slouch in recent months and wasn't keeping up.

And that was no assumption. If he was pulling his weight I wouldn't be getting flagged down by his grandmother almost daily. He used to be a pretty good kid. We saw him frequently, he went to school with Sarah. They spent a lot of time together, and he was her date for Homecoming.

I got hung up in my thoughts on that.

It had never stood out in my mind that the kid had watched the entire thing happen. I closed my eyes and sighed quietly for being so blind to it.

"What did you need, Lily?" I looked to her, her face looking up at me with eternal patience.

"Do you need to go, dear? I just wanted to talk and say hello, but I do have something if you have time. I don't want to trouble you."

"I always have time for you, Lily." I smiled down at her and she rubbed her hand up and down my forearm, patting the back of my hand with hers. Her face grew into a wide smile, full of wrinkles, that hid the warm kindness of her eyes in little slits. The glimmer that twinkled out from each of her wrinkled eyelids always curled my lips into a smile.

"Such a good boy. I missed you. Are you wearing clean underwear?"

I closed my eyes and laughed, tipping my head back before looking down to her again.

"Lily, yes. Of course, I am." Her eyes were twinkling up at me as we rounded the back corner of her home.

"Well, how am I supposed to know? You work such long hours and sometimes you don't come home. You have to take care of those things and bring extra."

"Thank you, Lily. I'm good."

The backyard of her home was well kept. A privacy fence all around recently repainted. I did a pretty good job, too. It was more flowers and shrubs than grass. Lily loved her big garden. It was more upkeep than she could handle though.

I was over here at least once a week just to help with that. Zero complaints though. Her vegetable garden was amazing. I wasn't allowed to work that, she refused help there. That was all Lily.

She grew more than enough for herself, so I always got baskets of fresh vegetables. Whatever was available in Michigan's short growing season.

I've tried talking her into letting me plant some corn, only because I love fresh sweet corn on the cob. She says it's a bother. Funnily enough, I'd be happy to help her tend it but I could never motivate myself enough to grow and tend it in my own yard.

I'd rather be here, I suppose.

I glanced up to the deck and saw Blake sitting in a folding chair with his feet up, smoking a cigarette. We made eye contact and he scowled and looked away.

"I'll be right back, Bobbie. Then I'll show you what I need you for out back here." She didn't wait for a reply. It was just matter of fact. Lily stated what was going to happen, and that's what was going to happen.

She moved slowly up the steps of the deck, holding the railing so tightly her knuckles went white. She seemed to be expelling a mountainous amount of energy to climb the steps, but she remained all smiles – eyebrows high.

Her hand went to Blake's shoulder as she moved past him, partly to steady herself, but partly to give him a loving pat as she moved through the sliding glass door into the home.

I stared at Blake from the cement pad of the drive, his gaze still fixed defiantly in another direction while taking a hit from his cigarette.

"Hey Blake, how have you been?"

"Good, I guess." His response was flat. His lips barely moved when he spoke.

"Listen…" I stepped to the edge of the deck, trying to find the right words not knowing his own emotional state around the subject. "I know you spent a lot of time with Sarah, and we used to see you a lot. I'm sorry I haven't tried to talk to you more. It's been tough. You're welcome over anytime I'm home."

He gave me a confused look, his mouth screwed up a little.

"Why?"

"I don't know. Hangout, I guess. I haven't touched my PS4 in ages, we could play some Madden or something."

"I don't have any reason to come over, remember? You killed Sarah."

He flicked the half-finished cigarette over the railing and out into the garden.

Standing 6'2", muscled, and fit, I can take a solid hit. I've wrestled psych patients twice my size with supernatural strength. I've been caught in bar fights. I played college football. I even got hit by a U-Haul truck on Southfield back in my younger days, when I rode a motorcycle.

Still, those three words hit me harder than anything ever has before. The raw simplicity of the statement, dripping with hate and malice. He said it like he was quoting a fact and had sources to back it up.

I reeled and felt dizzy.

You killed her.

A shitload of vile words started to well up in me, and I could see him trembling with the adrenaline of the situation. His face was flushed.

My lips moved to form words when the glass door slid open slowly. Lily toddled through the opening, all smiles, squinting at me with those innocent eyes. I choked the mouthful of vitriol back down and struggled to calm myself.

"Ok dear, I got your lunch." She moved to Blake and gave him a small plate containing a sandwich loaded with a generous helping of meat, cheese, and lettuce.

He never took his eyes off me as his hand closed over the plate.

"Thank you, Gramma."

His eyes were practically bleeding hatred. My jaw was clenched so hard my teeth were sore. Little fucking shit.

"Come on, Bobbie." She took my hand. "I'll get you some gloves back here. I just need some things moved."

"Sure thing, Lily." Blake and I kept eye contact a moment longer, scowling at one another, as Lily led the way. When her back was turned fully, Blake's hand rose, giving me a slow and steadily cocked middle finger before he stood up and retreated into the house.

*****

My eyes kept popping to the clock on the dash of the Grand Caravan. I shook my head as traffic crawled, sighing heavily.

"I'm gonna be fucking late again."

I could see the goddamn station towering over everything on the block; the clean, reflective blue glass windows giving it a modern, executive appearance. In the belly of the station was an expansive garage of equipment, bunk space, showers, lounge, and more.

There was a time clock at the heart of it, and that dick head was gonna be leaning against it.

59

I rolled my eyes back slowly as a tractor trailer was trying to back itself across the four-lane highway, completely stopping traffic at this point as it sunk itself slowly into an industrial parkway not two driveways before the entrance to HQ.

My phone chirped out the Old Spice whistle. Hunter was calling. I jabbed the hands-free button on the steering wheel.

"What?"

"Dude, where the fuck are you?"

"Sitting in the goddamn street watching a truck driver treat this load like it's his first time fucking someone in the ass.

"Oh, you're stuck in that shit. Man, Britski looks more pissed than usual. You're gonna be late Papa Bear, better get the fuck in here."

"Yup." I ended the call. The truck had put just enough of itself into the complex to allow my lane to start moving – and move it did. With every passing car people were honking, hanging birds out the window, and shouting obscenities.

We Michiganders don't absorb the kindness of Canada despite its close proximity. You definitely don't get any of it here Downriver. The company certainly didn't build its HQ here for the culture.

It was more for its proximity to the surrounding hospitals, along with its financial relationship to said hospital system.

I rolled into the drive and took the descending tunnel into the underground structure.

HQ, or Station 42, was a pretty impressive beast for the area. It was a private service, but the largest in southeast Michigan. HQ services twelve 911 contracts for municipal backup, including the City of Detroit, with crews spread out across a dozen stations throughout Wayne County.

Last night I had the pleasure of getting tossed on Station 9 – Downtown car. Today I could wind up any fucking place.

Wherever the living decide to try and make a transition.

I rolled through the parking deck, stashing the van and grabbing my gear. I was already late. There was zero point in hustling to the clock. He was already standing there – guaranteed.

I don't run, especially not for him.

Especially not today.

Posted from Station 42 meant BLS backups, psych transfers, and chasing shit all over southern Wayne County.

But that was normal, and normal was good today. Fuck Station 9, and fuck Sherry for putting me there.

I punched into the stairwell, finding Hunter on the other side of the door. He jumped back, having been reaching for the door as I came through.

"He up there?" I nodded as I passed him, climbing the steps. He fell in behind me.

"You know it."

"Truck ready?" My bag started to slide as I walked up the steps and I gave it a shrug, pushing the strap back up as I gave Hunter a sideways glance.

"Oh hell yes. You're gonna love it, too."

I stopped, nearly at the ground floor level and looked at him.

"Don't."

"Oh yeah." He grinned.

"It's the fucking..."

"Bariatric truck. We're hauling heavies." He finished my sentence.

"Are you fucking kidding me?!"

"Yes. C'mon."

"Oh, you mother fucker…" I shook my head, heading into the main office. The stairwell dumped you smack in front of the bunk house and attached lounge. Right outside the entrance was our electronic timecard system.

Nifty little device. Read the same cards we used for building clearance and all that shit.

Britski was propped against the wall next to it, staring at me as I came through the door. His head turned to look closely at the time on the time clock, then back to me.

The fluorescent lighting was making little white strips shine in his oily brush cut, that danced as he looked back and forth. I hated his stupid haircut, along with his stupid musketeer facial hair shit, and the goddamn white button down he wore.

Because every supervisor wore them.

White shirt bastards.

"You're late, Badger." His fingers went up and he curled one side of his stupid mustache. "Let's go talk in my office."

"Can we do that here? I don't mind a public flogging. I don't want to be late getting on the road." I pointed off randomly.

"Fine." He folded his arms. Dickhead.

This sell out spent the last eight years as a medic, milking every call. He smoked in his truck, treated patients like shit, fucked a ridiculous number of female partners over the years, broke rules, and overall was just an egotistical twatwaffle.

Unfortunately, he was smart as fuck and a good medic when he actually put hands on a patient. He also had a fucking business degree, so he grabbed an ops position.

Now he delighted in enforcing every rule and walked around the station with a thumb in his goddamn belt.

Who the fuck has a business degree anymore?

"How did your ambulance get shot to shit? Where were you posted?"

"Detroit," I said flatly. "Right where we were stationed."

"Did you tell a cop to fuck off last night?" He scowled at me.

"Nope. I told him to write me a ticket." I set my bag down, relieving myself of the weight. This was gonna be a while.

"Why did you leave exactly?"

I could see over his shoulder into the lounge. The heads of guys were starting to turn, glancing toward the door to see what was going to go down. Some were on standby, others either coming or going from shift. Any one of them would love to see Britski eat a fucking knuckle.

63

"Female patient, multiple GSW. Did that... thing where we go to the hospital."

"Don't get cute. You were ordered to stay on scene."

"I don't work for DPD." I cocked my head to the side, trying to stay relaxed. I was already feeling heated and had a thousand other things on my mind. I didn't need this stupid shit at the start of a 24.

"You don't have to go mixing it up with the department though. That's the kind of shit that costs the company a contract."

I closed my eyes and put my hand up.

"Here it comes," Hunter mumbled behind me.

"I don't give a fuck about the contract. It's my scene, I make the call. And I did. If you question that decision, then put me in for a review and we'll talk with ops and the board. Otherwise let me fucking clock in."

"Take it easy." He was firm, but slightly less of a dick – briefly. "I know your call was shit last night, and I know why. I'll let the tardy slide. Frankly I was considering sending you home. You need to talk, you bring your ass back to 42 and make it happen or take the day."

"Fine." I swiped my badge through the time clock.

*****

"At least it's a new rig." Hunter ran a hand lovingly across the dashboard. "Look, you can still read everything on the console."

64

There's perks to seniority. Having 12 years in, I was at the top tier of seniority. First pick of trucks.

582 was a newer truck, but she was getting serviced for a couple bullet holes and new windshield. We were in 611 today. And she was sexy. Parked outside the building, getting ready to exit the lot, I tapped through a few menus to get logged in on our tablet.

Britski popped out of a side door, looked around and spotted us. He jogged toward the truck, waving us down.

"Don't fucking do it..." Hunter mumbled. "He's gonna pull us out of this truck, I fucking know it."

I watched him approach and hit the power window button as he stepped up to the polished, gleaming rig. For a second I wondered how funny it would be to snatch him by his stupid mustache and roll the window up on it, letting him comically dangle as we drove around.

"Don't leave yet, you've got a third rider."

Hunter grunted quietly, and I swear I heard him choke on a curse.

"Student or new hire?"

"New hire. Royez. New basic, show her the ropes today."

"You're putting a basic on an ALS rig for a 24? Crash course. Nice. Welcome to the shithouse."

"She'll be out in a few. Sit tight, don't be an asshole."

Hunter leaned, snapping over in his seat. "She?" I could almost smell his pheromones.

"Don't. Be. An. asshole." Britski looked past me. "Hunter."

"Nah man, it's cool." Hunter rubbed the stubble on his head. It was usually so well shaved it had a nice polish and shine to it. He had some dark stubble growing back in though. This was our week for a couple back to back 24s with a night shift in the middle. By the end of it, like today, Hunter was pretty much done with trying to keep up appearances.

Except for now. He slapped his visor down and checked his teeth in the small mirror.

Britski shook his head and walked off, smirking and mumbling to himself. As he reentered through the side door he paused and stepped aside. A young woman, maybe early twenties, slid past Britski.

She was in a brand new, cleanly pressed company uniform that was straining to contain her breasts. They weren't huge by any means, she was just wearing at least one size too small.

Hunter was biting his knuckle.

"OH… my God." His hand went to my shoulder as she put a hand to her forehead to block the morning light. The gesture lifted her shirt some and made the fabric strain even more around her breasts. She paused and waved to us, increasing her pace to hustle toward the truck.

She was bouncy.

Her brown hair was put up in a ponytail, and it bounced and flowed behind her as she jogged toward the rig. Running past Hunter's door, she opened the side door and hopped in. She stuck her upper half through the pass through just as Hunter spun around to do the same.

I watched them nearly smash faces.

She let out a quiet squeak and laughed. "Oooooh, I'm sorry!" Her hands splayed out in front of her.

Hunter sat there staring at her, taking her in. She looked at him quietly and said, "Hi."

A grin slowly crept across his face. I knew that smile. Shit was about to get deep in here and it was going to last all shift.

"We're going now." I grabbed the radio mic and clicked the trigger. "Alpha611 to dispatch."

"Go ahead, 611."

An unfamiliar voice in dispatch. Sounded like a younger woman. I had heard we were getting a new dispatcher transferring in from some remote place in the northern sticks. Would be interesting to see how she did running dispatch in an urban sprawl.

Shit got a little more intense than cow emergencies and rolled over snow mobiles.

At least she responded quick.

"Show 611 in service, Ma'am."

"Copy 611. Sit tight. We may have a BLS call."

Aaaaand I hated her.

Hunter and I both slowly turned to look at each other and sighed.

"Copy." I tossed the mic down into the collection of Nitrile gloves between our seats. "I want coffee."

"Didn't you give Holly enough already?"

We grinned at each and I rolled forward, looking over my shoulder to see the Basic still hanging through.

67

She gave me a sweet smile. Pretty girl, curvy. I liked curvy.

Hunter LOVED curvy.

"You might want to settle into the jump seat. Telegraph is a little shitty this time of day. What's your name?" I rolled forward through the yard, heading for the exit.

"Sara!" she responded proudly.

I immediately mashed my foot on the brake.

The girl came flying through the pass through, landing on the console with a high-pitched yelp. Trying to catch herself, her hands set off a number of the lights.

The siren of the rig screamed to life, causing traffic just outside the yard to suddenly come to a crawl. I put a hand on her hip and rolled her toward Hunter, slapping at the switches to disengage the lights and shut down the siren.

Hunter caught her, his hands instinctively going to places that would let him cop a feel or four. He acted concerned, but his eyes said that he was fighting hard to contain his laughter.

Because that was funny shit, although unintentional.

She apologized profusely and managed to get on her feet. With one more apology she started to step into the back via the pass through. My eyes were still locked on Hunter. He was looking at me through watery eyes and struggling so hard to contain it.

I mashed my foot on the gas, the diesel engine roaring as the truck surged forward toward the yard exit. Another loud squeal and the EMT disappeared into the back. Hunter lost his shit, laughing loudly, and pressed his fingers into his eyes to contain the tears.

Maybe this wouldn't be such a bad shift.

Chapter 4 – Familiar Face

With eyes fixated on the windshield, half looking through it and at nothing in particular, I sipped the mocha latte. I don't often drink it at home much but I won't start a shift without some Timmy Ho's.

I just needed my coffee to get going.

Hunter on the other hand…

"At least we didn't catch that BLS call." I could barely understand him. He had a box of Tim Bits and was stuffing handfuls of the little donut holes into his mouth, chewing loudly and bobbing his head in excitement.

I didn't respond. I wasn't jinxing shit. I wasn't going to comment, or complain, or make a peep about the type of calls today. We were two hours into a 24 and sat posted quietly in an empty Sears parking lot.

Traffic rolled by steadily on Telegraph, punching through the city on six lanes of traffic. We'd seen four other rigs slip by in the last hour, so there were calls to do.

"It sure is quiet," came a soft voice from the pass through. Hunter's head spun backwards almost like an owl, his eyes wide. He had crumbs all over his uniform and in his lap, and a healthy film of powdered sugar rubbed across his chin.

"Get out of my truck," he said with a mouth full of donut.

I pursed my lips, shaking my head.

"What?" She looked confused and chuckled nervously. "It's really quiet… isn't it?" I had turned to look back at her and her eyes were bouncing between us.

"You fucked us," I said.

The tablet fixed to our console chirped to life as priority tones crossed the speakers. The screen populated with patient data as the tone echoed.

Hunter groaned at the radio and his eyes fell on our 3rd rider again, looking betrayed. "What did you do?!"

I pointed at the tablet and looked at her as dispatch rang over the radio.

"611 come back."

I grabbed the mic. "611 copy, go ahead."

"611 you have a priority 2 call, confirm."

Hunter held eye contact with the girl as his finger jabbed the button on the touchscreen, accepting the call.

"Confirmed dispatch, 611 en route."

"You." Hunter pointed a finger at her, with all the seriousness of a drill instructor, and bounced it slowly in her face as he shook his head.

He swallowed the last of the donut in his mouth. "You are so lucky you're cute as fuck."

*****

71

Hunter had read off the details of the call en route to the residence, which was just a few blocks from our post at the edge of Taylor. He only did that for the benefit of the 3rd rider. He may be a foul-mouthed horn dog, and likely fully intended to fuck this girl before end of shift, but he took his work seriously.

He always did a hell of a job with students, and he loved training. Smart and charismatic, that asshole had a gift for it.

Rolling up on the house, Hunter worked with Sara to get the cot, continuing to monologue procedures and throw her drill questions about what to do inside.

Snatching and shouldering the trauma bag, I lead the way through the door, greeted by a distraught woman. She was short and rather stocky, heavyset, fat. Whatever you want to call it.

Her cheeks were flushed but I couldn't tell if it was from exertion and anxiety or if that was the natural state of her otherwise pale skin – a little flush matching the red curly hair.

She was crying and pulling at my arm.

"He's back here, please hurry. He's so sick."

Hunter and Sara brought the stretcher in, and he instructed her to leave it in the living room. Following the woman, she led us into a small back bedroom where an older teen was sitting on the edge of a bed. Tucked into the sheets behind him was a young boy, maybe 6, quite pale and drenched.

"What's your boy's name, ma'am?" I turned back to her, offering a warm smile despite the situation. It was clear he was pretty bad off.

Flu maybe. Influenza was less likely in the spring, but still possible with how snotty and gropey little kids were.

"Bobby." She wrung her hands together.

"Oh, well that's my name." I smiled a little bigger to her. "My partners, Hunter and Sara, will take care of your son. I need to ask you some questions if we could step out and give them room."

Hunter nodded and slid past me with Sara in tow, and I passed the jump bag to him. He kneeled at the bedside and set about talking to the boy in hushed but energetic tones. As the older teen exited the room, hovering close to his mother to hang on every word, I could see the boy respond slowly to Hunter.

Lethargic, he barely had his eyes open.

"Ma'am." I clicked my pen, hovering it over my gloved hand. "Tell me when this started."

It was pretty much like I thought. The flu had gone through the house and had kicked around between the dad, mom, older brother and now the youngest, Bobby. None of them got vaccinated or saw the doctor. They had just let it run its course.

"Did you try treating it with anything? Is he taking any medications for this or anything else?"

"No… we didn't get any prescriptions." She shook her head vigorously, but seemed like she was uncertain of her answer.

"Anything over the counter – Triaminic, Dimetapp, Mucinex, Benadryl… chewable vitamins?"

"Oh, he took some Nyquil a few hours ago. He had trouble sleeping last night with all the coughing," she remarked and looked to read my face. I grimaced inwardly but didn't respond immediately. "Was that wrong?"

"Was it Children's Nyquil?

"Umm… no. I don't think so. We just buy the regular bottle for my husband.

"How much did you give him?" I continued to jot notes on my glove with the pen.

"Just a cup full, the little cup it comes with." She looked between her older son and me, like she was seeking validation. I nodded and stepped back into the room as Hunter rose, a serious look on his face.

"He's lethargic, weak pulse, pretty rapid. Shallow breathing. His temp is just over 104." His eyes were scanning the notes he had been scribbling on his own glove.

"Mom gave him Nyquil a few hours ago. Let's get him loaded up."

"Guys?" Sara drew our attention back down to the patient. He was starting to convulse in the bed.

"What's wrong with him?!" The mother was getting frantic in the doorway as Hunter kneeled again. The tremors were brief before his body went tense and rigid.

"Do you know if your son has ever had seizures before?" She shook her head, tears rolling down her face as she clung to her older son.

"Alright, we're going to take him to the hospital. I need you to ride with me, alright? Can you wait for us outside?" I put a hand on her shoulder and drew her attention to my face, trying to smile at her.

She nodded and choked on her tears, beginning to cry loudly as the older boy led her out.

"Seizure passed, probably febrile, but he's out." Hunter shook his head. "Something's off. Seems shocky to me. Let's go."

"Yeah, work in the truck. We'll go to Oakhill."

*****

I never had to question Hunter's skill. I knew he could handle anything that landed in the back of our rig. I trusted him without question. It helped that he had another set of hands back there. She might be a basic, but a good basic can be a hell of a lifeline on a call.

We weren't far from Oakhill – just a few miles. Coming up on midday I was thankful for the light traffic on US-24. I kept the majority of my senses on the road, with my ears trained to the back as I listened to the chatter between Hunter and Sara. I rolled to a light a few cars deep, waiting for things to start moving on the green.

It suddenly went quiet.

"What happened?" the mother cried out.

"Punch it, Badger!"

I didn't know why, I didn't care why. I reached down and threw on the side flashers and light bar, cranking the Whelen siren. The light was still red and the cars ahead of the rig started to turn and split from one another in an attempt to clear a path.

I mashed the horn and pushed the rig through spaces it probably shouldn't have fit through, crawling into the intersection as I rapidly alternated tones.

Hunter was barking into the radio in the back, reporting to the hospital as they worked frantically. It didn't sound good. The mother was wailing and begging them.

Luckily, we weren't far from the facility... just a few blocks.

Still, I rode the gas hard, weaving and bobbing in the ambulance around cars too slow to get the fuck out of the way.

"Hard LEFT!" I called out, giving Hunter a chance to grab the ceiling rail as I passed the hospital on the opposite side of the road, hitting the U-turn lane in the center median. A quick Michigan turnaround and the center of gravity shifted dramatically in the rig.

Sara yelped again. She knows what hard left means now.

Swerving around traffic I pushed the rig into the emergency entrance for Oakhill, shutting down the siren in the process. Rolling toward the ER bay there was a team of nurses and techs pouring out the doors as I spun around and backed in.

*****

76

Some crews transfer care and step out of the way, hands in the air, happy to lose the responsibility of the patient.

Hunter and I don't do that. We stay until we're told to leave. Dispatch hates it, but over the years we've earned a tremendous amount of respect in the hospitals we frequent because of that.

This time I wish I'd left.

The boy had coded in the back of the ambulance, and Hunter spent those brief minutes before arrival at the ER wrestling with death in the back of the rig. Surprisingly, he won the first match and got the boy breathing again.

We gave our hands to the team; whatever they asked, we did.

But it wasn't enough.

That boy coded four times before we were unable to hold him, and death took another before our eyes. It didn't hit me in that moment. I sighed and turned to leave and that's when the mother, standing outside the ER bay, heard the doctor call time of death.

She trembled violently and screamed. It transformed to a blood-curdling cry as she buckled and doubled over, wailing at the floor. As if screaming at the bowels of the earth would somehow set her son's soul free. That was when it hit me.

I had the same reaction when I realized Sarah was gone.

I paused and looked back to the boy's lifeless, pale body on the table.

The world had slowed around me. It wasn't some strange effect. I had just taken note that the pace of the room was suddenly much less frantic.

Why not... he was gone.

I felt a few gloved hands grip my arm and touch my shoulder as they passed. Touches of reassurance from nurses.

The mother appeared from behind me and lay on her little boy, wailing into his chest, sobbing heavily and squeezing him in her arms. I just stood there, watching. Reliving. The sound began to leave the room as blood pounded in my ears.

Hot rage mixed with a healthy dose of sorrow rose in my throat and my chin quivered. I closed my eyes took a deep, long breath.

You lose one more. One more down.

A deep breath again as I tasted bile. I swallowed hard.

How many more?

"Bobbie." A whispered name. I didn't know if it was mine or the boys. A gentle tug at the fabric of my uniform shirt made me blink slowly. My eyes were dry and burned as I blinked. I had been staring hard, eyes fixed on the poor mother. She was weeping more quietly now.

I turned to find Hunter cocking his head toward the hall, gesturing for me to follow. I obliged, silent and hollow in the moment. My head felt like it was filled with helium, my tactical boots full of lead. In that moment, I realized the room was empty save for me, watching over the woman as she mourned the loss of her boy.

She killed him. Just like Sarah was killed.

78

Hunter had the tablet and was standing at the counter, watching me as I emerged from the room. Our 3rd rider turned around and looked at me. It was Sarah.

My Sarah.

I closed my eyes and felt sick. Opening them again, Sara and Hunter were looking at me with eyebrows raised in slight concern.

"Bobbie, you ok?"

The call hadn't rocked Hunter at all. If it did, he didn't show it. He might never show it. We might talk about it tomorrow, next week, or never.

Even the 3rd rider stood, unshaken, her eyes still innocent and unchanged. She had seen some shit during her clinicals and ride alongs. Enough to not be phased, but not enough to strip the innocence from her eyes.

"I'm good."

So not good. So far away from good.

"You sure?" Hunter stepped to me and slapped me on the cheek lightly. "Gonna be a long shift, man."

"Yeah, hell of a way to start it." My face was grim. "But I'm good."

What's the opposite of good? Evil. Yeah. Murderous and evil.

Our phones chimed a notification almost in unison, mine was a quiet chirp. Hunter's started playing the Imperial March. Dispatch notification. He had his out before I moved to grab mine.

"Looks like we're heading back to HQ." Hunter tucked the phone into his breast pocket and turned, firmly grabbing a handful of the 3rd rider's ass. "C'mon beautiful, let's see if we can salvage the day." She blushed hard and batted at his hand with very little effort, bouncing along after him with the freshly prepped Stryker cot. I watched them head toward the exit of the emergency room before glancing over my shoulder.

The curtains we're pulled for privacy in the ER pod. No noise came from the other side. If there were any life left in the distraught mother, it had been all but drained from her. A nurse slipped by me into the room and, with a polite smile, shut the door behind her.

*****

Mark and Ella were waiting for us in the pit bay at HQ, a quick drive through point for accessing the main offices, grabbing supplies, etc. without having to navigate the entire yard and garage. Why our HR leads were greeting us was beyond me, but it didn't sit well.

More bullshit about the fucking DPD altercation last night. It was always something.

As long as it wasn't about Sarah.

I couldn't take one more person asking me if I was okay.

The HR duo stepped up to the driver's side window as I rolled it down.

"Ella. Mark. What's up?" I hung an elbow out the window and leaned out, turning the rig off. The diesel engine knocked briefly before shutting down, letting the sound of traffic roll in as it echoed off the building.

"There's a detective here to speak with you, Bobbie. Can you come inside?"

"Uh... yeah." I was caught off guard by that, immediately going back to the most recent calls. What the hell would a detective want? I didn't think my nerves could tighten any more, but they were winding up like piano wire.

The anxiety was nearly strangling me, and it must have shown.

"You've got access to company legal with your benefits, Bobbie." Ella cocked her head as she stepped back, giving me room to hop out of the ambulance. "You need us to call anyone for you?"

"No, I'm sure it's nothing. Thank you." I looked back to Hunter in the rig. "I shouldn't be long, brother. Just sit tight."

*****

Over the years I've learned to trust my gut. The few times that I didn't listen to that gut feeling, I usually got myself in trouble.

My intestines were knotting up hard when I walked into the conference room. The HR duo had only escorted me that far, then left.

I was alone in the expansive room.

81

Some two dozen chairs sat neatly tucked under the long table. The room was rarely used, I think. Either that or someone deserved an award for their attention to detail in cleaning. If more hospitals were this clean we could likely eliminate all the secondary infections people caught during recovery. The whiteboards that lined the walls looked like they had never been touched. The dark oak table was highly polished, gleaming and reflecting the fluorescent lights back upward.

An oversized analog clock hung on the wall, out of place among the modern tech and clean wood, tapping loudly with each second that passed.

The latch rattled and the door opened, breaking the heavy weight of silence in the conference room. I turned to look, met by the cheeky grin of Nick Farzo.

My old partner from the days when we were basics. The wop bastard had tried for medic at least a half-dozen times and repeatedly bombed the national registry tests.

He eventually gave up, left EMS, and went the law enforcement route.

Last time I had seen him and his wife, we were burying Sarah. I didn't speak to them though. I didn't speak to anyone. It had been years since I really spoke to Nick.

"Hey, Bobbie. How you been, man?" He stepped in, shaking my hand hard and slapping my shoulder. He was about as cookie-cutter Italian-American as you could get. With double-breasted suits, you could put a fedora or black homburg on him and swear he was a mobster straight out of Goodfellas.

I was decidedly more relaxed at seeing a familiar face and felt tension start to melt away. The room felt far less constricting in its sterile state as my hand closed around Nick's.

"Same shit, different day. You know how it is, Nick."

"Yeah, no shit, B. No shit. Sit down, man." He yanked a chair out and dropped into it, looking around with a whistle. "Ain't been in this place in a long time, man. We we're just basics back then, huh?"

I smirked and sat across from him at the table, nodding.

"Yeah, look at you now. Detective." I made finger quotes. "That's big stuff, Farzo. How's the wife?"

His big black eyebrows went up. "Fucking pregnant with twins, can you believe that shit? She's as big as a bull and just as mean."

I gave him a genuine smile, sighing inwardly as relief seemed to wash away with each second that ticked by on the giant clock behind Nick.

"That's terrific, congratulations." I shifted back into the chair, relaxing more. "So, what's up? What are we doing here?"

Nick shifted as well, mirroring my actions and rubbed the dark stubble around his chin.

"Bobbie, I gotta ask you some questions about this morning. What were you doin' before you came in to the station today?"

I shrugged and started to rattle things off.

"I came off shift and had breakfast with Hunter downtown. You know the old Coney over by Greek Town." He nodded and grinned a little. "Eggs still taste like shit by the way." We both laughed.

"After that I went home. Holly was there. We hadn't seen each other in a while so we talked about some things. Had a bit of a tiff, spent the morning trying to work out some stuff."

"Yah, I get like five of those a day from mine," he responded with a knowing nod, but he wasn't looking at me. He was writing in a small steno pad as I spoke. "How is Holly anyway?" His eyes looked to me, genuine concern being worn openly

"She still kicks my ass." I smirked again.

"We missed you at the New Year's fundraiser for Children's Hospital. Holly looked good. I talked to her a little while ago, she said you guys had a fight this morning. You all left at the same time?

"Hunter came over to ride in for our 24 today. Holly left before us." I leaned forward in my chair. "What's this about, Nick?"

He clicked his pen and balled a fist, resting his chin on it as he looked at me.

"Got a call this morning about a possible domestic over by your place."

I sighed and rolled my head to the side. "We were loud but I didn't think we were that loud. It was just some arguing, Nick. Nothing happened. Usual shit. You know how Holly gets."

84

"Nah, not on you." He waved his hand dismissively. "Not you and Holly, anyway." I stared at him, my brow curling in confusion.

"What are we talking about then?"

"Local PD responded and found your neighbor in her backyard. She was tagged pretty bad. Someone worked her over good."

"Who? Which neighbor?" I leaned forward, staring hard at him, my stomach twisting. I think I already knew this answer.

Nick glanced at his notes then back to me. "Lily Merriam-Beecher. Talked to some of the other neighbors, couple said they saw you with her this morning. Said you looked a bit hot when you left."

My eyes went to the table. I scowled as my eyes darted around, searching for something to help process what he had just told me.

I shook my head and looked back to Nick, his eyes staring at me with his eyebrows raised slightly.

"Jesus, Nick, you don't think I killed her…"

One more down. Another one down? How many is there gonna be today?

Nick looked a little surprised as he arched an eyebrow.

"Who said she's dead?" His eyes stayed locked on me.

"Well, is she alright?"

"It's pretty bad. She's old, probably won't make it. She's over at Oakhill Main. Not responding and she's circling the drain." Nick tapped the pen on the table as he watched me. "Anything you want to tell me?"

"Fuck, Nick, I'm at her house almost every day. I've been helping her with odds and ends for a while now." I wrung my hands, feeling the piano wire of my anxiety wrapping around me, cutting deep. "She asked me to move some boxes in her garage. That's it."

"Hunter stick around for that?"

"Shit…" I rubbed my forehead and could feel sweat was starting to bead on my skin. "No, she called me over and I told him to go ahead without me to get the truck ready here at HQ."

I watched him take more notes.

"This wasn't me, Nick. You know me. I'm a fucking medic for Christ's sake."

Nick cut me off, putting his hands in the air.

"Bobbie, relax. I'm not charging you with anything. No one is saying you did anything. I'm just following leads trying to get information."

I huffed incredulously, scratching my head as my eyes stared off. My thoughts went back to this morning, and I remembered Blake.

"What about her grandson? Was he ok?"

Nick's eyebrows went up. "Who's her grandson?"

"Blake Wheedon. I saw him there this morning. He and I had some cross words about… Sarah." I stumbled over saying her name, more than usual.

"Lotta that going on this morning. Rough shift?"

"Something like that."

86

Nick scribbled again before looking to me. "No sign of family at the house. Didn't even know someone was staying there with her. Just her in the backyard."

I gave him more details on the kid and our relationship with him, right up until the altercation that morning. I kept shaking my head, struggling to process the idea of what happened to Lily.

And just after I had left her.

That's your fault, too.

"Okay." He let out a sigh and stood, straightening his suit and tucking the pad away. "Sorry you had to hear about it like this, B. I'll probably have to circle back at some point. Might have more questions for you."

"I'm on shift till the morning, Nick. You know where to find me."

*****

The cold water splashed across my face, stinging against the heat of my flushed cheeks. Vertigo came in waves as I held myself over the sink.

I splashed the water again, rubbing my hands around my face. Salty saliva began to flow, filling my mouth. I tasted metal and felt my stomach heave. I spit into the sink, taking a deep breath, and letting it out slowly.

Rising a little, I looked at myself in the mirror. My eyes were wide, a little bloodshot. Bags were starting to form. I still couldn't remember the last time I really slept. I couldn't even remember my last meal.

Why Lily? Why today?

Today is the perfect day.

I was angry. I had just been there. If I had called off and stayed home I would have wound up in her garden most of the day. I could have been there.

I couldn't save her.

And now she's going to die.

My stomach rolled again and I hunched over the bathroom sink, dry heaving hard.

A few hard knocks on the door echoed in the private bathroom adjacent the conference room.

There's so many I couldn't save.

"Badger," Hunter called through, somewhat muffled. "We got a call, buddy. Everything okay?"

I splashed another handful of water at my face again before snatching a wad of towels to dry off. Staring at myself in the mirror I stood with water dripping from my nose, hanging off my dark facial hair.

I was watching myself age.

Not often did I actually feel like my age. I felt a hell of a lot younger than almost forty. But not now.

Drained is a good word for it. I felt absolutely, completely, drained to the core.

How many more are we going to get today?

"Fucking peachy."

*****

The scene was a clusterfuck when we rolled up on it.

88

I was in place to take the call, scanning the info we had on the tablet as Hunter pushed us toward the incident, skillfully rocketing us through traffic like a professional race driver.

I'd seen him do things with an ambulance that would slam your asshole shut.

Pucker factor of 9.

My mind was all over the place trying to process the shit from the last few hours. Adding a multi-vehicle collision was not going to make this shift any easier.

Scanning the scene as we rolled toward the intersection, PD was already controlling the flow of traffic and two other crews were working among the mess of mangled cars, including guys from the local fire department.

"Looks like they're extricating on that one." Hunter pointed as he parked the rig in the middle of the intersection of Telegraph. Several firefighters were using hydraulic jaws to cut open the driver side of what looked to be a Challenger… didn't look much like it anymore. "Look at those fucking cars, man."

Glass and pieces of various vehicles were spread across the intersection. Probably a blown signal; someone ran a red. I counted four cars, and each looked like they had been through a destruction derby.

"I want the backboard and immobilization gear – it's the blue bag inside the bench." I looked back at the 3rd rider as I gave her the instructions before snatching up the mic for the radio. "Alpha611 on scene."

"Copy 611, show your arrival."

89

"Let's grow some wings." Hunter stuck out his fist to me and held it up. He was grinning. Despite losing his last patient he was fine.

He probably wasn't fine. Not inside. Not with all the shit we've seen. But it rolled off of him for now.

I bumped fists with him and smirked. He loved the comment about growing wings. Something he saw in a movie. He liked the idea of swooping in and saving people. There was still that little bit of trauma trooper left in him, though he kept it controlled.

He made a little explosion noise after the first bump, throwing his door open and leaping out.

God love him, he kept a smile on my face no matter what the fuck was going on.

*****

Hunter walked through procedure with Sara behind me, explaining to her in detail what the first responder crew was doing. We stood at the ready just off to the side as we waited for them to get us access to the patient.

The car was crushed like a can, with a significant portion of the engine compartment compressed. The sides looked like the car had gotten T-boned from both sides. City fire already had a C-collar on the patient in the driver seat to stabilize her spine.

One of the firefighters had wedged himself into the backseat, holding her head still while talking to her.

90

All the other patients were accounted for and handled by other crews. One of the first responders supplied me with the patient's vitals; she was actually fairly stable with no obvious injury – just extremely shaken.

The older boy that was in the backseat wasn't as lucky, and would probably be in critical condition the way they described his injuries to me. One of the rigs was already gone, having transported that teen.

Now we just needed to get to mom.

"Clear!"

"We're clear!"

The tools we're handed off and the last hunks of twisted vehicle were moved aside. We moved up with our gear to get the patient to the backboard.

God bless city fire. The woman already had an IV in place, oxygen, and was remarkably calm. It was one of the smartest choices the city made a few years back to require all firefighters to be licensed paramedics.

I stepped into view of the woman and leaned in, smiling softly to her.

"I'm Bobbie, I'm a paramedic. I don't want you to try to move, including your head. If I ask you a question, just sit tight. and answer me with a yes or no. We're going to get you out of here now and over to the hospital with your son. Alright?"

She didn't budge at all except to look to me, her eyes making contact with mine. Her long brown hair was wet and clung to her face – sweat and tears.

She looked familiar.

Makeup was running around her eyes. They were puffy, with abrasions across the side of her face.

Airbag caught her, she was lucky.

"Can you tell me your name, the year, and where you're at right now?

"Uhh.. Lisa. It's 2017… and I'm in deep shit." She chuckled a little as a tear fell down her cheek. At least she was trying to make the best of it.

"Lisa, I've been doing this a long time. I've never seen anyone look as good as you in a tough wreck like this. We're gonna take care of you." She smiled a little and watched me with knowing eyes, sniffling. "If you feel any pain at all when we start to move you, I want you to tell me. Alright?"

"Okay."

"These are my partners, Hunter and Sara. They're going to put a vest on you to protect your back while we get you out of there."

"Okay." Her voice was shaky now and tears were running steadily down her face.

The fire crew gave us room to work, with the one remaining in the backseat continuing to stabilize the patient's head and neck. I prepped the backboard on the stretcher as Hunter and Sara secured the patient to the KED board.

Even with zero complaints of pain, she needed that full immobilization. Too many patients have suffered permanent and debilitating spinal injury to risk trying to move her without that extrication device wrapping her torso.

It only takes a slight twist to paralyze someone, and they may never feel pain.

92

Zero fuck ups happening today. None.

Not losing any more.

I was still tense as fuck, and the hairs stood up on my neck despite everything about this call being textbook. I just kept waiting for the other boot to drop. I felt myself clenching my teeth as I watched Hunter, Sara, and the first responders slide her from the driver's seat onto the backboard to lay her on the stretcher in one fluid motion.

Fucking flawless.

God, I love you, Hunter.

I clapped him on the back as we strapped her in place, transferring her to a non-rebreather mask on our own oxygen tank. The bag on her mask was inflating and deflating slowly. She was still calm, steady, and a quick check of her vitals immediately after moving her showed she was good.

Even her tears had settled.

"Alright Lisa, you're doing great. We're gonna take a quick ride down the road to the ER."

She muttered a response that was clear agreement, but muffled by the mask covering her face now. She likely would have been fine with the nasal cannula the responders had given her.

Zero fuck ups. She gets all the oxygen I can give her without forcing it in using a bag valve mask.

Despite her condition, my tension continued to increase. There was a lot of chaos at the scene still. Another crew had shown up and was yelling back and forth to other crews as they ran around looking to assist.

Not sure who it was but they were making a fucking ass of themselves.

Hunter and I loaded the patient in, and I slapped the 3rd rider on the ass before pointing to the jump seat behind the patient's head.

"Just observe for now. I'll take the patient." I climbed in behind her. Before Hunter had a chance to close the rear doors, someone hopped up on the bumper and stuck their head in.

"BAAAAADGEEEER! What's UP man?!" he screamed loudly, scaring the patient as she let out a gasp and small scream of her own. I spun around, finding one of the basic EMTs that had been running around the scene. They were trying to find someone to help so they could get their piece of the action.

He was standing on the bumper, hanging on the doors, grinning at me stupidly.

"Need some help, dude?!"

Didn't know his name, didn't care to know his name. He had only been with the company about six months. Another goddamn trauma trooper. How the fuck he knew me was beyond me.

Using the rail in the ceiling, I lifted myself and kicked at him. I used all my weight to plant a foot firmly in his chest, sending him flying off the bumper. He tumbled out and landed on his back on the pavement.

Hunter just stepped aside and watched him drop before looking at me.

"We good?"

"Yup."

He shot me a thumbs up and slammed the doors shut.

*****

As far as calls go, that was about as easy as they come without taking a basic life support call. We didn't get pulled for BLS backup often, but when we did it was either a welcome break from chaos or a complete pain in the ass.

Most of the time it was a complete pain in the ass.

It was rare to get a 911 backup like this – something this easy.

I'm sure the patient never feels this way. It's a monumental fuck up for them. One minute you're heading for work, and the next minute your battered body is lying in a hospital bed. Car is totaled, you're not getting paid for missing work, your kid is hurt…

Different perspectives. I should feel more for them, but after twelve years the mundane shit like this doesn't even move the emotional needle.

Just the fucking shit calls.

After transferring care to the ER staff, I stood outside the patient's pod, finishing up my paperwork at the nursing station. Glancing around I found Hunter getting the stretcher setup with fresh linen.

He was wooing the girl.

I could tell because his lips were moving.

She was also grinning and turning a half dozen shades of red.

95

Her nipples were also hard.

Yup. They were gonna be fucking by the end of the night.

"Do you have a fucking problem?!"

Someone bellowed from directly behind me and I turned.

Gerardo. That skeezy fuck of a Paragod.

I know he wasn't talking to me like that. I was ready to lay his ass out.

If ever there was a piece of shit that didn't deserve to wear the uniform, it was that fuck. This asshole went from basic to paramedic in school without ever working the road. He acted like he knew it all, but had one of the largest complaint files on record at HQ.

Most of which were from hospital staff complaining about his fuckups prior to transferring patients. How he still had a license, or even continued to work for us, was beyond me.

Gerardo has a few inches on me and was a tall son of a bitch, but was lanky and barely a lick of muscle. Just a big, douchey, overgrown asshole.

"What the fuck is your malfunction?" He was barking down at Ramirez, a short-in-stature basic EMT about half his size. She was looking up at him like a child with her hand caught in the cookie jar.

I stared, curious over the exchange. A little drama in the middle of the ER was always a nice distraction, but not from this guy. Heads were turning all over and ER staff were scowling at his volume, tone, and choice of language.

"You don't touch my drug box. You don't look at my drug box. You don't even think about this drug box. You don't need to go anywhere near it. Keep your hands off my shit, you're just a basic." He had inserted himself between her and the stretcher holding the drug box in question.

Ramirez put her hands up, looking a little nervous and confused. "I was just trying to stop it from falling off your cot."

"If it ain't yours, don't fucking touch it!" He bent and barked into her face.

"Hey, Gerardo!" A redhead walked up and pushed the EMT back behind her with the care and protective demeanor of a mother bear. It was Plevoska.

I loved Plevoska, mainly for the fact that she hated everyone in the entire world. She readily admitted it, with one exception.

She loved her partner, who was now peering out from behind the voluminous red locks of hair.

Plevoska was casting a shadow over her smaller partner.

She stood even with me in height and had an impressive stature with broad shoulders. They build them standard like that in Russia. She wasn't Russian of course – at least not as an immigrant. Just the genetics.

She scared the shit out of me though, and that takes a lot.

Plevoska squared right up to Gerardo, pushing her tits into his chest and getting right in his face, looking into his eyes.

"Do you have a problem with my basic, you no-talent fuck?"

I leaned on the counter of the nurse's station with one elbow. This just got more interesting.

The ER was still a flurry of activity, but everyone was doing their best to pay attention to the exchange.

He started to speak and she put a palm up to his face. "You know what? Don't. It doesn't matter. And let me tell you why it doesn't matter." She put a hand on her hip, still practically nose to nose with him.

"That basic right there is mine. Unlike you, I've been in her boots. I waded through the same shit she goes through, and I have had to put up with the same stupid, ignorant shit that you're slinging at her. I've been there. And you know what? Someday that girl is going to stand in our boots. At least I hope so."

She thumbed over her shoulder as she continued to bark into his face without discretion.

"That EMT has my back. That EMT does my CPR. That EMT starts my IVs. That EMT cares for my patients better than half the medics in this company. And that EMT," she turned slightly to point at the young girl that was standing just behind her. "That EMT is my mother fucking partner."

"You don't bark at my EMT. You don't command my EMT. You don't shit talk, degrade, question, belittle, or swing your dick at my EMT. You don't ignore, or discount, my EMT. You sure as *FUCK* don't discourage my EMT or make her feel like she is any less than the rest of us."

He started to speak in response to her and she put her palm in his face again, silencing him.

"I say she's *MY EMT* not because I'm the medic on the car, and she's just a basic. But because that's my EMS sibling. After countless 12 hour shifts of granny stacking and shit slinging, I am the only one who has earned the right to give her shit, and she has earned the same. That EMT has always had my back, has never let me down, and never will. Because that EMT is my partner."

Save for a few people moving about, most of the ER was now standing still and watching. People were like mannequins.

Plevoska moved closer, practically nose to nose with him. He moved to step back and bumped into his stretcher

"I need my EMT. And you sure as fuck will respect her. Because if you don't, I'm going to park my boot so far up your ass, every thought you have is going to have to dance with my toes before it leaves your punk-bitch mouth. Clear?"

He didn't respond, choosing instead to stare at her with wide eyes.

Maybe it was less of a choice and more of an instinctual response to ensure survival.

"I know it's hard to speak with my cock in your mouth, so I'll just assume you agree."

His face had lost quite a bit of color and he slowly looked down, hanging his head. Plevoska tugged on the sleeve of her partner before walking around him and heading my way. Hunter stepped up next to me slowly, his mouth hanging open. Plevoska was scowling hard and glanced to us.

99

"I love you," came out of Hunter's mouth as she walked by.

She sneered at him and kept walking. "Shut up, idiot."

Hunter turned slowly and watched them walk by. He stared hard, eyes fixated on her. I watched him briefly before glancing after them. Just before they turned the corner, Plevoska looked back making clear eye contact with Hunter. A little smirk appeared on her face as she disappeared, served up just for Hunter.

"Welp. She wants me." He clapped his hands together then rubbed them furiously. "I'm gonna go see if she'll suck my cock."

He made a gesture and all the noise of a sloppy blow job, complete with gagging, as he walked away. Sara laughed and he snagged her by the elbow, pulling her along.

"C'mon wingman, she likes basics. You're gonna get me laid."

"I'm wrapping this run report up, I'll be done in a few." He didn't hear me, and even if he did he didn't care. When there was no patient to tend to, Hunter was hunting for a place to park his dick after shift.

I turned to see Gerardo looking at me as he distractedly adjusted the belts on his cot, pouting and acting like an indignant child.

"Making friends, Gerardo?" I gave that asshat a toothy grin.

"Fuck off, Badger."

*****

My fingers punched out the text to dispatch as we sat in the parking lot of the hospital, holding before we called clear from the run.

"What are we doing, man?"

"Getting some food, hopefully. I need to eat. Trying to get dispatch to let us go invisible but I don't know who's working." I finished out the text and hit send. "Now we wait."

A short request to go invisible was sometimes allowed, usually after a call like this that takes a while. As long you didn't abuse the request, dispatch would try to leave you alone long enough to get a meal in before dumping a call on you.

Unless it was a 911 response, you were usually safe. In the last 12 years, I've requested to go invisible maybe five times. Each request has been granted, but then again that was dispatchers I knew.

The unfamiliar female voice came over the radio. "611."

I sighed and picked up the mic. "611, go ahead."

"Copy you 611, your request is cleared."

Hunter gasped and put a hand to his mouth dramatically.

Sara slid up between us through the pass through and looked confused. "What does that mean?"

Hunter stuck his chest out and thumped it, grunting loudly, bellowing in a raspy voice. "It means we're gonna eat some real fuckin food!"

Chapter 5 - Wings

I couldn't remember the last time I had put hot food in my face. Getting the opportunity to sit down in a restaurant, in the middle of a shift, wasn't exactly uncommon.

Over the years, we'd sat in plenty of restaurants trying to catch a meal.

Being there long enough to actually see and taste your food was the rarity. I couldn't count the number of meals interrupted by priority calls. After a while you just stop trying, and start living off shit you could eat in the truck.

I needed a change today, and Hunter deserved it.

He was hunched over his plate, shoveling heaps of ketchup-covered hash browns in his face. His shoulders sagged a bit as he chewed and he exhaled a long sigh through his nose. Sara sat next to him in the booth, the 3rd rider picking at a platter of fruit.

It felt good to sit and not feel rushed. My food didn't really satisfy me overall, but it stopped my stomach from trying to eat itself. One less thing to distract me.

Hunter washed the mouthful down with a long gulp of his coffee, then looked around the restaurant.

"I love Ram's Horn. I love the coffee. I love the food." Hunter smacked the table. "I even love this booth. You know why? Cause it ain't that goddamn Coney you love, and there's no one here talking shit and ruining my food."

Just over his shoulder I watched her saunter up quietly, a shit eating grin on her face. I clenched my jaw to avoid ruining the surprise with a grin.

"I add most of the flavor to your food, sugar." Cindy bent down and blurted it out right next to Hunter's face. He jumped sideways, driving Sara into the dividing wall of our booth.

"No! NO! How are you here?!" Hunter grabbed the salt from the table, shook some into his hand, and threw it at her. "What are you, a fucking wizard? Jesus Christ…" He slid slowly back to his place in the booth seat, glancing back to her more than once with a scowl.

Cindy laughed good and hard, the deep laughter riding out rumbles in her chest that told the tale of decades of heavy smoking.

Sara was rubbing her side and shifting uncomfortably at the assault from Hunter, but it looked like it was more for attention. She might as well have been wearing a sign around her neck that said "Hunter, put it in me."

Cindy leaned against the corner of the booth's high back, slapping Hunter on the shoulder playfully. "Darling, you know I'm just foolin'. I was here having lunch with my girlfriends and I saw my favorite boys. It's like a hobby for me now, Logan."

His eyes went up to her, showing tolerance alongside frustration, but you could see genuine appreciation for her. Hunter liked Cindy, deep down. No matter how much he complained.

"You should try something more productive, like jogging."

"Hmm, I don't know. The only reason I'd start jogging is so I could hear heavy breathing again."

"Ugh…" Hunter slid his plate forward in disgust.

This is normal. This is absolutely normal.

Normal was supposed to feel good.

So why did I feel so absolutely hollow? I felt empty, void of anything save for the partially eaten Reuben sitting in front of me. Where a grin was fought back on Cindy's arrival, there was zero emotion now.

Humor felt far away, not quite as in reach as sadness. There was no tension, but an ever-present feeling of anger – like a pot kept constantly just below the point of boiling over.

I sighed and looked up, catching Cindy's eyes on me.

"Bobbie, will you walk me to my car, darlin'? Carry my leftovers for mama." She put her hand out and stuck her nose up in the air like a debutante that was to be escorted.

"Sure, Cindy." I slid from the booth and tugged at my belt line, adjusting and tucking in my uniform shirt. I set the portable radio down hard in front of Hunter. "I'll be back. You two should talk more, it's kinda *quiet*. Hunter's buying."

"Wha-… oh… you son of a bitch."

*****

104

I was reaching for the door to head back into the restaurant, my focus a bit of a daze as the sound of Cindy's voice beat around in my head. Hunter and Sara popped out before I could close my hands on it, the tones for a priority call blaring from the radio in his hand. We all paused as he held the portable up, staring at me.

"I hate you. I just want you to know that right now."

"You got your chance to eat." I took the radio from him and clipped it back on my belt, the three of us quickly walking to the rig. "What did we get?"

"Unresponsive female at Veteran's Metropark, caller is a kid. PD's en route." Hunter opened the rear doors for Sara, grabbing a handful of the 3rd rider's ass as she jumped into the truck. He looked to me with a grin before splitting off to the passenger side. "I really like this one. I'm gonna keep her."

Hunter confirmed the minimal call information on the tablet. Child made the 911 call, reported parent unresponsive. Unknown cause, unknown time down, practically unknown everything.

That's usually not a good sign. Maybe we'd get lucky and this was one of the hero kids you see in your Facebook feed with a couple million shares about how she saved mommy from choking by being quick to call 911.

I shook my head as we pulled out of the Ram's Horn parking lot into midday traffic, gunning the engine. Hunter looked at me, and I glanced at him. His eyes darted around as the ambulance picked up speed.

105

"Bobbie?"

He fucking talks too much.

"What?" I looked to him again as I started weaving around traffic.

He reached over, one eyebrow curling, and started flipping console switches for the lights, the siren coming to life. Cars began to part, opening up a channel down the center of the five-lane road.

"Lights and woowoo, baby. We don't want to be causing accidents today."

I didn't respond to him, I just kept my eyes forward. I could see him studying me a moment longer from my peripheral vision. It aggravated me. More than it should have.

He seemed to be staring for an eternity.

I felt words welling up from deep inside

What the fuck are you staring at? What? What? What?

It was an uncontrollable urge to bark at him. I felt hot and angry suddenly. I huffed in a hard exhale and was about to speak when our 3rd rider leaned up from the back.

"Is it like this every day? There's so many priority calls." She had to raise her voice a bit to be heard over the wail of the siren.

I didn't respond. I just pressed the horn to make the siren change tones, stepping up the frequency as I picked up speed.

"Woah..." Hunter's grip tightened noticeably on the tablet, his knuckles went white as I shot through the intersection. I blew that red. It didn't dawn on me until he reacted.

106

I didn't let on that I had fucked that up and Hunter seemed reluctant to say anything. I could see him looking at me again. He finally turned his attention back to Sara.

"Yeah, for ALS crews. We get a lot of the 911 stuff and ALS transfers for pediatrics, people going out to level 1 facilities with meds hanging in their IV, stuff a basic can't touch because of the medical controls." He was looking at me again.

Stop fucking looking at me like that…

"So… as a basic, I wouldn't be on priority calls?"

Hunter smiled and looked back to her. "Nah, you'll see a fair share. Basic crews run backup for ALS, and you'll catch some 911's. Probably have patients tank on you in the back on a routine transfer, too. Plus, depending on your station assignment, you could wind up on a medic/basic car. They see a lot of shit, especially when they cover big events downtown."

I changed up the siren again, blaring the horn. At least he stopped looking at me. His infatuation with our 3rd rider was restored.

"So, what do you usually do to wind down after a shift like today?"

Hunter turned more in the passenger seat, leaning over the arm and giving her a toothy grin. Their faces were inches from each other the way she was propped in the pass through of the ambulance cab. "Baby, I go home, take my clothes off, and watch a movie with my girlfriend."

"Oh, you have a girlfriend?" The disappointment in the poor girl's voice was obvious and dripping.

107

"Nope. You wanna come over and watch a movie after the shift?"

"Sure!" she blurted out. Charming son of a bitch.

That snapped me out of my daze. Suddenly whatever fog was encompassing my brain was lifted. I looked at Hunter, and he looked right back at me.

"Wassup, boo?" His eyebrows went up.

"That was smooth as fuck." I grinned and stuck my fist out. He bumped it, throwing his hand out and open as he made an explosion sound.

Sara chuckled from the pass through between us, grabbing the backs of our seats to brace herself as I turned the rig into the Metropark.

*****

Most of the little Metroparks were empty during the day, especially this early in the spring. It was still chilly, and upkeep on playgrounds was kept to a minimum. This was one of the smaller Metroparks in the area, which I appreciated.

I wouldn't have to drive around a few different two-tracks trying to locate the potential patient.

If there even was one.

Wouldn't be the first time a truck ran on a 911 to a Metropark only to get jacked for their drugs. It didn't matter that a kid had placed the call. Junkies will use anyone and do anything to get their fix.

Even stab a medic, just for some morphine.

A bit of my tension eased as we rounded the turn of the only drive that circled the park, spotting a single vehicle next to a pavilion.

There was a little girl in a colorful hoodie, grabbing at the arm of someone slumped over on a picnic table. She was shaking them hard and hitting them. Her face turned to look our way as we rolled up. You could see her face was bright red, her mouth open as she screamed unknown words.

She looked like she was maybe ten.

Fucking calls with kids.

I can't do more of this today.

Hunter unbuckled and dove through the pass through as I rolled up and parked. He grabbed the Zoll defibrillator and had Sara grab the jump bag. Before I could put the rig in park he was already leaping out the side door with Sara close behind.

The girl was screaming still, standing next to the person at the picnic table, tears streaking down her face. She kept screaming, "Momma!"

I broke into a sprint as soon as my boots hit the ground, following behind Hunter. He and Sara had the patient leaned back and lifted, lowering her to the ground. Dropping opposite Hunter, I prodded Sara to tend to the child as I dug into the jump bag.

"Not breathing," Hunter said. "No pulse."

Sara led the child away, the screaming subsiding a little as we went to work. I pushed with an aggression I hadn't felt in a long time. It was less anger and more passion.

We'd lost enough in the last 24 hours, I wasn't letting her go.

Not another single fucking patient today.

If death showed his face right now, I'd square up and say 'Fight me, bitch.'

Hunter moved to check and secure the patient's airway. He shot me a quick thumb in the air as her chest rose with the first squeeze of the bag valve mask. I immediately began compressions, feeling cartilage and bone crack and separate within her chest with the first few compressions.

"I thought PD was supposed to be here." Hunter looked around while working the mask on the patient, driving air into her lungs. He looked back to me. "Easy, Badger. Easy. Too hard, brother."

I tried to ease the pressure I was applying, but was driven. I didn't feel like I was in control, but I knew I couldn't stop. A siren grew in the distance rapidly, the sound of stone and dirt popping under tires.

"Took 'em long enough." Hunter looked over my shoulder, continuing the delivery of oxygen. "Oh shit. It's Holly!"

I blinked and stopped compressions, looking over my shoulder. "What the fuck?"

"Bobbie!" Hunter slapped my shoulder, and I looked back, then down to the patient. I scowled and continued compressions.

Hunter slid over, gesturing to Holly. She had sprinted toward us and dropped into place over the patient's shoulders, taking over the rhythmic squeezing of the bag that delivered oxygen to the patient between rounds of compressions.

I turned my head, locking eyes with Holly. Sweat ran down my nose, pooling and dripping from the end of it.

"Hold up, Bobbie."

I rocked back on my knees, breathing heavily. I wiped the sweat from my face on my shoulder and pulled the shears from their pocket on the leg of my trauma pants. With a quick motion, I cut a clean slice down the length of the hoodie the patient was wearing, working with Hunter to place the leads across the patient's body, running to the Zoll monitor.

"Get the cot. Get the cot!" I barked to Hunter as I placed the last of the leads and defibrillator patches, reaching across to grab and turn the Zoll so I could see the screen.

My eyes watched the peaks bouncing across the heart monitor, consistent, looking like a row of M's. Paper started to spit from the portable monitor.

Pulseless ventricular tachycardia. She wasn't dead, but she wasn't far off either. Something was disrupting the electrical signals in her heart, causing it to rapidly misfire. Her heart was beating so fast, the chambers didn't have time to fill before the heart would contract.

I dialed up the defibrillator to 200 Joules. Hunter came back dragging the stretcher and knelt opposite me with the drug box from the rig.

111

"Pulseless Vtach. I'm gonna shock. Clear." I looked to Holly and met her eyes again, and I swear to God I heard her voice in my head say 'you can do this.'

"Clear, Holly. Shocking in 3."

I punched the button, her body jerking slightly as muscles contracted under the electrical shock.

"No change." Hunter shook his head at the monitor, immediately resuming compressions. "Holly, oxygen." She replaced the mask on the patient, giving a solid squeeze as Hunter finished a round of compressions.

I dialed the Zoll up to 300 Joules and let it charge.

"Charging. Get Clear. Shock on 3."

Holly's voice rang clearly in my head again and I looked to her quizzically. She was watching me.

You've got this.

Punching the shock button again, the patient's body went rigid, her arms and legs jerking a little more than the first shock.

"I've got a good rhythm, Badger!" Hunter checked for a pulse, nodding. "Weak as shit but we got her. I need to stabilize, get her on the cot."

In the back of the ambulance I got a clean line for Hunter, plugging in a bag of lactated ringers. A glance out the back and Sara was with Holly, loading the little girl into Holly's cruiser.

I called out the open back doors of the rig.

"Let's get moving, Sara!"

Holly snapped to attention and looked to me, then to our 3rd rider, some of the color leaving her face. I felt for her in that moment, because I knew the exact kind of gut wrenching torment hearing that name just brought her.

I looked back to Hunter.

"You good?"

Hunter nodded without replying, his hands were working over the patient. He spun open the oxygen in the truck and switched the supply off our portable bottle to the nozzle in the truck wall.

My hand squeezed his shoulder and I turned to step out. His hand caught mine and I glanced back.

"Your wings look beautiful, baby." Hunter winked at me and gave me a wry smile before he continued using the bag valve mask to provide oxygen to the patient, breathing for her.

I smirked and jumped out, pausing for Sara to hop into the back with Hunter before closing the doors.

*****

It had been hours since I'd had a cigarette, and the craving was hitting me hard today.

That poor kid, screaming, mom not waking up.

Fucking torture, not knowing what was going on, no one around to help. Thank God, she thought to use mom's cell to call 911. No doubt that one was going to show up in the news in a day or three.

It would make its rounds on Facebook, too.

113

'Little girl finds mother dying. You won't believe what she did next.' It would read. Fucking clickbait. Likely not much mention of anything we did. She would be the star in the story.

After enough time passes you get used to being a faceless, nameless entity. It always has been and always will be a thankless fucking job.

At least calls like this made up for a lot of the shit ones.

I had been sitting on the rear bumper of the rig, leaving those two to deal with the cot and giving their report to the ER team. Popping the pack of Camels from my breast pocket, I lit one and leaned forward with my elbows on my knees. My stethoscope swung from my neck and I watched it, wishing it could hypnotize me enough to bury some of today's bullshit.

The cigarette brought more relief than I expected.

It probably had something to do with the call. A save lifted a lot of weight, but it was just a bandaid.

I honestly didn't think she was going to make it.

Another rig rolled up hot, killing its sirens as it came down the lane toward the ER bay. Sinking the rear end into the bay by the doors, the crew burst out of the truck greeted by hospital staff. The lot of them disappeared as fast as they had arrived, one of them standing on the edge of the low bars of the stretcher doing chest compressions on a patient as he was rushed inside.

I took another hit, closing my eyes and slowly letting the smoke out through my nose.

"There you are."

114

Holly.

I was hoping she would find me out here, yet dreading it at the same time.

"Where's the kid?" I looked up to her.

"With social services inside." She stood opposite me, hands on her hips. "You look terrible."

"It's been a morning. You stole my naptime." I looked up to her, squinting a bit at the sun gleaming behind her. It gave her a glowing silhouette – almost like an angel – eclipsing her so I could barely see her features in the glare of her halo. I thought she was smiling at the comment but couldn't really tell. "Did you hear about Lily?"

She scoffed and her posture relaxed "Yeah. What the fuck, Bobbie? Was that Blake?"

"I don't know." I flicked the cigarette. "He bit my head off this morning right after you took off. I was helping her with some stuff. I guess it happened shortly after I left for the station."

"You saw Nick then."

"Yeah, I got pulled into HQ, he talked to me." I took a long hit on the cigarette, rolling it between my fingers. Another ambulance rolled in – city fire this time. "It's madness out there today."

"Yeah, I've been running, too. Everyone is tied up. That's how I ended up on that Metropark call."

"It was good to see you." I looked up at her again, trying to smile with a hand to my forehead to shield my eyes. I wanted to see more of her face.

115

"I missed you, too, baby." She stepped sideways a few paces to give my eyes a break from the light. She read my mind. "You really look exhausted, Bobbie. You gonna be okay?"

"I wish people would stop asking me that today."

She stood there quietly a moment. My eyes were locked on her shoes now. I suddenly felt like I didn't want to look at her.

"You did good with that patient." She was trying to make me feel better. Backpedaling a little I guess. "That was the way I remember you. I could see it in your eyes, you were so focused. I liked seeing that Bobbie again."

"I haven't gone anywhere, Holly. Always been here."

I lied.

Fucking gone.

"I worry about you, baby."

"You shouldn't. I'm fine." I flicked the last bit of the cigarette and stood, brushing off my pants and looking down at her with a slight scowl.

"Yes, I should. You're my husband. It's my job."

"It wasn't your job when you walked out on me?"

She stared coldly at me. The look of hurt on her face was obvious. Despite being a trained killer and formidable woman, I succeeded in crushing her.

"That's not fair, Bobbie. What about this morning?"

"What about it?"

"I thought we were going to work on us. I thou-"

116

"You think because you show up at my house, and I fuck you, that we're just going to be okay? You thought you could take off on me, fucking destroy me, and then just come right back... like what? Like nothing happened?"

"Bobbie... no, I d-"

"You can fuck right off with that. I don't need that pressure right now."

I lied again. Every second since this morning that her and I were apart I felt myself slowly decaying from the inside. There was a steady flow of blood from someplace deep inside, and it only stopped when she was with me.

But I was so... fucking... angry.

Fuck her, don't need her.

"Oh." Her face hardened and her jaw went rigid. "Okay then."

I expected her to walk away angry.

Or fucking hit me. I deserved that much, not even going to pretend otherwise.

Instead she stood there quiet for a moment before she spoke.

"Will you still call me after your shift... please?"

I closed my eyes and hung my head. God bless this stubborn bitch, I really did need her to balance me.

My eyes rose to meet hers. She wasn't angry. In fact, her eyes were pleading. Practically begging.

"Yeah. Yeah, okay, Holly. I'll call you. We'll talk. Just not now."

"You did good with that patient, Bobbie."

She was trying to cheer me up. She probably knew better than anyone else how dark my thoughts had been today.

I could only force a smile at her. Whatever barrier kept me from saying it was still there. It reminded me of this morning. How badly I wanted to show her that I still loved her.

All I could muster was a nod as I shifted my stance, crossing my arms over my chest.

"I'll be fine."

She touched my forearm and smiled, squeezing it slightly before walking away toward her cruiser parked at the opposite side of the ER bays. I watched her go, feeling a part of me leaving with her.

The hollow feeling was returning.

Fucking idiot.

My phone chirped a notification.

Pulling it from my pocket, I read the text from dispatch and scowled.

'STAT return to HQ when clear.'

What now?

*****

"That was the guy who had the exploded scrote! You remember that, Badger?" Hunter slapped at my shoulder as he drove us back to HQ. My face was resting in my hand, an arm crossed over my abdomen. My gaze was fixed on the dash, staring at the molded, textured surface intently.

My mind was elsewhere. I hadn't heard him.

118

It didn't register that he had been telling Sara another story. He had been at that all day, impressing her with our war stories. It was working, too.

She was enamored with him.

He swatted at my arm again and I blinked, looking over to him.

"What?"

"That call. The guy with the blown-out nuts."

"What about it?" I scowled a little, feeling irritable. We made eye contact and Hunter's shoulders dropped a little. He just stared at me, with a very serious and concerned look.

"You know what… fuck HQ." He snapped his turn signal up and slowed down, pulling into a large shopping center. A car behind us locked up its brakes to avoid kissing the bumper of the rig.

The driver pulled around, continued to honk their horn as they passed.

"YEAH yeah… I got the right of way… fucking… asshole. My road." Hunter mumbled and slung the ambulance into a corner of the lot. He put the truck in park, shut it down, and opened his door.

"Out. Now." He jumped out of the driver's seat. I watched him walk around to stand in front of the ambulance. He was staring at me, raising his arms with palms to the sky.

I popped my seatbelt and hopped out, joining him. My hand went to my breast pocket, searching for a cigarette.

"Not you, beautiful." Hunter pointed over my shoulder as Sara walked up from the back. "Sit tight in the back for me. I got other plans for you." He winked and put his hands on his hips, looking back to me.

I lit the cigarette with my zippo, flipping it closed with a flourish and stuffed it into my shirt pocket.

"I'm just gonna come out with it, man. I've been with you six years on this truck. I've seen you run days without sleep, go without eating, piss out of both ends when you were sick. I like to think I have a certain unique perspective on what makes Bobbie Badger think and act the way he does."

I took another hit and exhaled slowly. "Okay. And?"

"So, all the shit we've seen I've never seen you like this."

"I'm just tired."

"Fuck you, man. Don't feed me bullshit. I deserve better than that. Fuck that noise." He stepped back and paced a second, crossing his arms. "I've seen you tired. I know what a sleepy fucking Badger looks like."

"I don't know what you want me to say, Logan."

"I want you to fucking talk to me, Bobbie. You're scaring me."

I looked down at the asphalt of the parking lot. Cracked, deteriorating out here at the corner of the lot, bits of stone and pebble scattered all over from a thousand patch jobs.

Everything in me felt strangely similar.

Aged, patched over, not weathering time well, flawed and getting worse.

I gave him only silence as I smoked. He just stared at me. *Stop fucking staring at me.*

120

"Hello? Dude, after that call last night with the Sarah lookalike," My eyes jumped up to meet his and I scowled again. "THAT. That shit, right there. Right fucking there. Ever since then you're coming to pieces."

He started ticking off on his fingers.

"You ain't you, you ain't on the ball with the patients today, you blew that red light doin' fucking 65 easy."

"Don't talk about her."

"Well, someone has to. Shit, man. I don't want to fucking die today because you've got your head stuffed up your ASS! Look at you. I know it's a lot. I can't even imagine that weight, and then you got Holly in your shit, too – and I'm sorry about that. That was my bad for calling her."

Hunter stepped closer to me, putting his hand on my right shoulder, gripping it firmly.

"Bobbie. Seriously. I see you sitting in a dark place right now. You ain't gonna make it to the end of the shift like this."

I'd had about enough of people asking me if I was okay. I took a hard drag on the cigarette as I felt rage start to rise.

It didn't have to go far. I continued to carry the feeling of a pot already at the boiling point. My nerves were on fire. My face felt hot.

I exhaled and took another hit on the cigarette before tossing it and looking at Hunter.

"Here's what you're gonna do." I crossed my arms against my chest, my eyes settling on his. "You're gonna get back in the truck. You're going to drive us back to HQ so we can figure out what the fuck is going on."

121

"Bobbie…"

"And I swear to God, if you talk about my daughter or that call last night one more fucking time… Logan. That's it. You can find another fucking partner."

I turned to climb back in the rig, glancing to him as I opened the door. He was still standing in front of the rig, scowling at me.

"Get in the fucking truck, Logan." I climbed in and slammed the door.

He put his hands up and shrugged, shaking his head, and made for the driver's seat.

There was a dead silence in the rig as he turned the ignition, the diesel engine rumbling to life. Neither of us spoke or looked at each other. Hunter hesitated putting it into drive and he sat there staring at the dashboard a moment.

The 3rd rider emerged from the back through the pass through.

"Everything good? I hope I didn't mess up." I could see her looking between us. Neither of us moved. "It sure is quiet all the sudden."

I closed my eyes and sighed as the tablet almost instantly triggered, filling the cab with the sounds of priority tones. I let a single huff of air escape my nose. It was about all I had in me at that moment.

My eyes looked over to Hunter.

When we made eye contact, I started to grin. Just a little.

"Fuck." He laughed and turned to look at Sara with a twisted brow. "Darlin, you are hella smart, absolutely gorgeous, and I can't wait to take you home later." He looked to me then back to her again.

"But goddammit I hate you right now."

I looked at the call info on the tablet's screen.

"Light it up, it's a kid." I punched the confirmation button and brought the radio mic to my face.

"Dispatch, 611 en route."

"Copy 611, show you en route."

*****

You can't let the names of communities deceive you in the Downriver area. Most of them sound like upscale, newer subdivisions. In reality, it's just one expansive trailer park after another. I try not to judge the residents or assume much about them based on where they live. It's hard not to though.

Especially when they look like Center Pine Estates.

It was a two-mile deep park filled with aging single-wide trailers sitting smack in the middle of what would be the shadow of Detroit Metro Airport. We rolled through the lane-and-a-half wide streets of the park laid out like a grid, passing one broken down, disheveled car after another.

Most of the homes were missing siding, skirting, and even windows – which were now covered by duct tape and cardboard.

The unit for our call had a particularly large amount of debris and scrap stacked around outside.

123

I counted at least six lawnmowers – which was amusing given the complete lack of grass.

It wasn't the first time we had been in this trailer park, and it wouldn't be the last. It was usually for overdoses, domestic violence issues, med seekers. A pediatric call like this was actually pretty rare here.

We bailed out of the truck and grabbed our gear, moving with the same speed we would give to an affluent patient from a wealthy community in Royal Oak. Not all crews made an effort to stay blind to the shit.

Just one more reason why I appreciated Hunter.

I tried to push the argument out of my head, but it was eating at me – along with everything else. Between Holly, Hunter, and what happened to Lily, I had to admit that I was struggling with focus.

The last thing I needed today was another pediatric call, and we headed for the door expecting the worst.

'Baby not acting right' is about as vague as you can get, but that was all dispatch had for us.

Climbing the steps with the gear, I raised a fist to knock and found the door ajar. With a few raps of my knuckle, the door swung in slowly. The smell that hit me made me reel. It was a mix of rotting meat, old garbage that had been left baking in the sun, animal shit, and ammonia.

"Paramedics!" I tried to breathe through my mouth as much as possible as I called out inside. The door was pulled open from within.

A guy in a dirty wife beater and greasy pants, matched only by the grease in his hair, hung on the top of the door… likely to keep himself upright.

"Oh hey." His eyes were glassy, and he looked every bit the part of a textbook meth user. "She's in the back."

"Can you lead me back?" I looked to him, mentally struggling to keep the scent out of my nostrils. "What seems to be wrong with her?"

"I dunno. She ain't doin' much. She usually cries a lot. Figured something was wrong."

His breath smelled like he had been feasting on shit sandwiches. His teeth – the few he had left - were mostly rotten, black, and broken.

I stepped inside, my eyes scanning for a path through the small single-wide trailer. It was impossible to see the floor for all the trash.

There was *so much trash*. If there was anything of use in the piles of garbage, there was no way to tell it apart from what was generating the odor.

I'm pretty sure everything was generating the odor.

He turned and staggered, stepping slowly through the trash in the living room to the narrow hallway leading us into the back of the home. Hunter put a hand on my shoulder to keep himself steady as we navigated the refuse.

Sara made it two steps into the home and gagged, doubling over. She quickly backed out and ran outside.

"We're good without her," Hunter said as he slapped my shoulder before lowering the volume of his voice to a whisper. "She doesn't need to be in this shit."

I was high stepping around piles of takeout food bags and batting at flies that zipped by my face like they were dive bombing me. The guy stopped at the last door in the hall, pointing inside the room.

"She's on the bed. You guys want a beer?"

"Nope. Thanks." I pushed past him. We entered what I assumed was the master bedroom and it was, thankfully, a lot cleaner. Still filthy, still stagnant, but at least you could see the floor.

Unfortunately, the floor was nothing but exposed subfloor and there was animal shit scattered everywhere.

There was no way this kid was coming back to this house, I'd make sure of that.

In the middle of a half-rotten mattress and box spring, sitting directly on the floor, was a little blonde girl. She looked to be about a year old. Honestly, she could have been as old as two but she was clearly underweight. Borderline emaciated and probably starving.

She was nude, her entire body covered in bright, angry rashes and what looked bed bug bites. They covered her nearly from head to toe. Some of them were open sores, weeping blood-tinged fluid.

There was old, caked on fecal matter around the inside of her thighs and all over her hands.

Despite all of that, the little girl lay on the bed staring at her hands quietly. She had blue eyes that looked like they were capturing all the color of a spring sky. So alive, curious, innocent, and oblivious of the hell she was born into.

She was silent. Not upset or crying. But she didn't make any noise either. She just continued to play with her fingers as we came in.

"Jesus Christ..." I stepped to the side of the bed and looked it over. The bed bugs weren't even trying to hide. They were crawling all over, in and out of the soiled sheets. I looked to her again and you could see them crawling through her wispy golden hair.

That's when she looked at me. She had heard me speak.

Nope.

Her eyes looked to mine and my stomach rolled over. It felt like a cauldron full of molten steel had spilled inside me.

Done.

That heat began to grow. I couldn't move. We just stared at each other. Her hands raised up and pointed toward me, fingers wrapping around each other. She made a little sound like she was trying to blow bubbles.

Let's add just one more.

I turned and pushed past Hunter.

"Bobb-..Bobbie where are you going?" He spun as I walked past. "Hey. Hey! What are we doin', Bobbie?"

My boots kicked straight through the trash, pushing up swarms of flies and other bugs. There was no careful placement of my steps. I marched back through the living room. The guy was leaning back against a dining room table covered in takeout boxes, beer bottles, and empty cigarette packs.

As I approached him, he just stared stupidly at us. He never really saw me coming.

I picked up one of the old wooden chairs at the table and lifted it. With a quick spin I brought it down across his head and shoulders.

"Bobbie! STOP! WHAT THE FUCK ARE YOU DOING?!"

The chair exploded into pieces as the guy groaned and fell back onto the table. I let go of the pieces of chair in my hands and grabbed him by the neck with my left hand.

I didn't count, I just kept swinging. I didn't feel anything, and if it weren't for all the blood, I don't think I would have known that I was connecting. All I felt was white hot rage inside me. I felt like my arms were steam vents, releasing pressure continuously and out of my control.

Hunter was still yelling at me, trying to grab my right arm, but I kept swinging. It took him crawling onto my back to set me off balance and release my hold on the guy. We fell back together into the piles of filth.

The guy slid off the table and collapsed to the floor. He was struggling to breathe, blood gurgling in his mouth as he wheezed and gasped.

I started to get up to reach for him again when Hunter wrapped an arm around my neck and put me in a submission hold, wrapping his legs around my waist.

"BADGER!" he bellowed in my ear. "FUCKING STOP!"

The first thing that came back to me was the smell. The realization that I was down in the middle of all the garbage with Hunter clinging to me with everything he had. I could taste bile.

My hand was throbbing.

I saw the guy laying there, covered in blood, and it dawned on me what I had just done.

Sara appeared in the doorway, brought by the commotion, a hand over her mouth to fend off the smell as she looked at Hunter and me, then to the bloodied guy nearby.

I struggled to get up but Hunter held me firm, choking me a little as he fought to hold me. I put my hands up and relaxed.

"I'm good," I croaked out.

He hesitated but started to release the hold slowly.

We crawled to our feet, stumbling in the piles of garbage. I brushed old, slimy food and maggots from my trauma pants and looked down at the guy. Sweat was running off my face, but I dare not touch myself. I was panting heavily, the blood pounding in my ears.

Hunter stood there, equally winded from trying to control me. We both just stared at the guy on the floor.

"Sara, call for another unit." Hunter didn't look at her. He didn't take his eyes off the guy. She nodded and disappeared outside.

"Badger."

Holy shit.

"Badger…"

Is he still breathing?

"Badger!" Hunter grabbed me by my bicep and jerked me toward him. I blinked and looked down at him. We stared at each other and I realized I had never seen that kind of shock on his face before. He was scanning my face and clearly saw something in my eyes that spooked him.

"I... I don't know."

He hadn't asked a question, but I knew what was going through his head.

What the fuck were you thinking?

It was going through my head, too.

One more today wouldn't make it worse.

"He jumped me." Hunter said, looking me square in the eyes. "He jumped me while I was questioning him. You came out and worked him over to get him off me."

"Hunter..."

"Shut the fuck up and listen." He clenched his eyes at me. "You're fucking done if this gets out. Go with it. Just fucking go with it. I'll cover you."

I nodded slowly and looked down at the guy on the floor. He was still alive, but his face would never look the same again.

"Yeah... yeah ok." I nodded again.

"He probably fucking deserved every swing," Hunter muttered. "Just sit tight and make sure he doesn't fucking die I'll get the kid while we wait for another unit and PD."

"Yeah."

"Bobbie... "

130

"Yeah?" I looked to Hunter again, feeling a bit dizzy. Almost drunk, or like a rush of endorphins was washing over me.

I felt good.

"Are you square?"

So good.

My eyes wandered, trying to process the question before I scowled a bit and looked to him.

"Yeah…" My mouth hung open and I sighed. "Wings are gone though."

*****

Hunter was dealing with our 3rd rider, likely making sure that whatever she saw, or thought she saw, was in line with exactly what he wanted the world to believe about the incident. I sat in the EMS crew room of the hospital, hunched over the table in front of me trying to finish my report on the kid.

Unfortunately, it was the first time I'd ever put myself in a position of hiding the truth when writing up incidents. It was creating a mental block that made it impossible to focus.

Other crews were passing in and out of the crew room to wrap reports, talk shit, grab a drink, etc. A few I hadn't seen in a while exchanged fist bumps and handshakes. It felt like every one of them saw right through me.

They knew what I had done, and they knew Hunter was throwing lies to save my ass.

I felt absolutely tainted.

As if I had just assassinated my own character.

There was absolutely zero chance at recovery. You don't come back from that.

The other paramedic crew who responded to back us up were awestruck at the condition of that guy. Even the responding officer who took our statement said he'd never seen anyone worked over like that.

Not for one second did any of them even think to question the validity of our story. As far as they were concerned, I was protecting my partner.

'Watching my brother's back,' the cop said. 'That's how it's done.'

One of the other medics said he was surprised I didn't kill the guy. He would have.

I tapped at a few of the check boxes on the touch screen, filling in data on the child to complete my report. Every time my thoughts went back to the call, and writing the details of the patient, my anger rose again.

He fucking deserved it.

The social worker had already gotten details on what we found at the home. There's no way that baby would be going back into his care. God only knows where the mother was. God, the nurses had murder in their eyes when they saw the child as well. No decent human could see a child like that and not be furious.

Most people don't start swinging chairs though.

I felt overwhelmed and out of control. Exhausted. Every time I turned a page it was just another emotional experience. Every call was cutting deep into me today.

I signed off the report and docked the tablet, feeding the patient info into the central database at the hospital and printing off duplicate copies for end of shift.

That seemed light years away. I checked my watch.

2:40 p.m.

Christ, I had at least another 18 hours to go and that's only if we got off on time. Not bloody likely. There was always one more last minute call that would suck an extra hour or three from your soul.

A notification triggered on my phone again.

Another text from dispatch to return to HQ.

"Would have been there already... make up your mind."

Chapter 6 – Mass Casualty

We dropped the rig in the pit bay and left the 3rd rider to clean up the truck, restock, and organize in our absence. I had a feeling we might be here a bit, given whatever topic needed to be discussed stacked with assaulting a civilian.

Or self-defense. Whatever.

That was going to create a headache of paperwork and internal investigations.

No HR duo to greet me this time, so that was a bonus.

Pressing through the offices we made for Britski's little slice of heaven. Having already dealt with him once today I was at my quota for the week. I wasn't looking forward to listening to his mouth again.

Not today.

His door was shut. It was symbolic of his outlook as a white shirt bastard supervisor. Need to talk or vent? This is the last doorway you want to try to darken.

Britski isn't exactly the "lean on me" type. He's more of the "hold my beer while I jerk off in your face" type.

Hunter thumped on the door with his fist while looking at me. "I want to get out of here, dude. Just keep it chill okay?"

I shrugged at him.

"You don't have anything to worry about with me. I'm chill as bare tits on a figure skater."

That couldn't have been further from the truth.

I wasn't exactly intimidated by Britski. I was more terrified of what it meant to hide the truth. I'd known for a long time that this job changes you, at the very deepest and most intimate parts of yourself. You stop becoming whoever you used to be and grow into something a lot colder, darker, and apparently… unpredictable.

But there was zero desire in me to sacrifice my moral compass.

The door swung open and Britski stared at us before stepping out and shutting the door behind him.

He nodded with his hands on his hips, looking at me then to Hunter.

"You monkey fucks. What the fuck did you do?"

Hunter jumped to speak but Britski shut him down.

"That was a rhetorical question, you ignorant fuckwit. Do you realize the shit you've stirred? Between dealing with these detectives and the goddamn ops and medical director, I haven't stopped getting my ass hammered all afternoon."

Hunter couldn't resist the opportunity.

"Don't you like it in the ass though?"

"What detectives?" I stepped on his remark, but I needed to know more with all the shit going on this morning.

Britski didn't respond to Hunter immediately. He thumbed over his shoulder while looking at me. "They're waiting for *you* inside." He clapped a hand around the back of Hunter's neck and grinned as he stepped aside.

135

"You and me are gonna go talk about insubordination while you organize the supply locker."

The two wandered off down the row of offices, Hunter glancing back with a look of concern. I threw him a simple salute to let him know it would be fine and wrapped my hand on the knob, stepping into Britski's office.

Nick Farzo turned around from his seat in front of Britski's desk, giving me a forced smile and a nod. I paused in the doorway and looked to him, then to the other body in the room. He was standing at the window behind Britski's desk with his back to me and hadn't moved.

Same kind of dark hair as Nick, bigger build though, like me. His clean black suit and obvious chiseled build was a pretty hefty contrast to Nick's lean mobster-style getup.

"Nick. Didn't think I'd see you so soon again today. What's up?"

"Hey Bobbie. Have a seat." Nick stood and slid his chair sideways to face the other situated in front of the desk. I stepped in and shut the door, my eyes going to the man at the window who stood like a statue staring out the open blinds.

It was stupidly melodramatic. Britski's shitty office faced the road. So, unless this guy had a hard-on for watching cars roll by, he was just trying to play the room. I settled into the seat and brought a foot up across my thigh, resting my hand on the side of the polished black boot.

"I appreciate you talking to us, Bobbie." Nick released the buttons on his coat and flared it open, sitting with his elbows on his knees so he was leaned toward me. Open, relaxed, chill. I put my arms up in a little gesture to mirror his open body language, nodding to him.

"Whatever I can do, Nick. Who's us?" I looked to the other guy and back to Nick.

He finally turned and looked at me through the shades he was wearing. A hand went into the pocket of his suit pants.

"I'm Carter. I work with Nick in Homicide."

His introduction was as flat and stoic as he could make it. He and Nick shared a lot of the same Italian-American characteristics. Whatever else Carter was mixed with though, he was a big son of a bitch, with shoulders like a linebacker.

Like a fucking Viking dripping with machismo.

Even with a clearly tailored suit, the fabric still strained to contain his arms.

"Did you find out more about Lily?" I nodded to Carter after he introduced himself and looked back to Nick.

"That's what we wanted to talk to you about, Bobby. Just some questions. I don't want to take you off the road too long, I know you catch a lot of bad shit out there."

"You got lunch today at Ram's Horn." Carter interjected, stepping on the end of Nick's statement.

My eyes went back to him and I shrugged, nodding.

"Yeah. Hunter, myself and the 3rd rider with us today."

"Why that one?" He was still wearing his sunglasses, a deep tinted black that matched his perfectly pressed suit.

137

"Why that what? That restaurant or that Ram's Horn?"

"That restaurant. Specifically."

"Hunter wanted to eat there. He won't shut the fuck up about their coffee."

"At that specific restaurant." Carter stared at me, his hand still in his pocket.

"Yes. At that specific restaurant. He even picked the booth – Nick, what the fuck kind of questions are these?" I looked back to Farzo, giving him a confused scowl.

"Take it easy, Bobbie." Nick put his hands up toward me. "Carter got brought in to work with me on the case."

"Wait, you said Homicide?" I looked between the two of them. "What the fuck happened to Lily, Nick? Is she dead?"

"She is." Carter stood up and slid the glasses off, tucking them into the inside of his jacket as he stared at me with hard, black eyes. "And someone else."

"Fucking shit, who? Nick?" I looked back to him, my foot thudding to the floor as I sat up.

He sighed and paused while staring at me. He knew her just as well as I did. We'd spent plenty of time there back when Nick and I worked basic life support.

"Cindy."

"Fuck you! Is this some kind of fucking joke, Nick? I just saw her. I *just fucking saw her.*"

I could feel that searing anger rolling up again, the blood was pounding in my ears. Adrenaline was coursing through me and I could feel my stomach turn. It had been a while since I felt that familiar fight or flight rush of adrenaline.

My body was starting to tremble.

"It's not a joke, *Badger*." Carter put a little extra emphasis on my last name, almost with a mocking tone. "I have witnesses that saw you exit the restaurant with the victim. Those same witnesses all had stories that put you leaving the restaurant in a hurry not long after."

"We got a fucking priority call, of course we left in a hurry."

He settled back against Britski's desk, placing his palms down on the surface behind him as he faced me.

"Why did you leave the restaurant with her?"

"Nick, this is starting to sound a lot like you're accusing me." I ignored Carter's bullshit question, my eyes burning towards Farzo.

"Bobbie, they're just questions. We have to follow every lead, it's just routine shit, man."

"Do you want a lawyer?" Carter stepped on Nick's statement again. I saw Nick give Carter a pursed lip glance. There was some tension there, so they obviously weren't on the same page.

I had a dark feeling this motherfucker thought I was a murderer.

"Are you charging me with something?" I shot back at him.

He shook his head once and looked at me.

"Nope."

"Then we're fucking done." I started to rise from the seat, Nick reaching toward me to say something but Carter reached out and put a hand on my shoulder first.

"Not quite."

Our eyes met and it took all I had not to try to lay him out on the desk for putting his hands on me. I felt the familiar swell of rage coming back, like the last call and that fucking meth head.

I settled slowly back into the seat and looked at him.

"Do you make it a habit of attacking your patients?"

This motherfucker.

"I didn't attack the guy," I said flatly, staring at him cold.

He smiled slightly and nodded. "Well, I'm glad we both know exactly who I'm talking about."

Shit.

"I had no choice."

My entire fucking world spun as I made that statement. That was it. I lied. It didn't even feel like my voice when I said it. The words seem to come from someone else, like a ventriloquist making me speak.

"Oh, I'm sure. That's what I heard. Protecting your partner and all." He stood and folded his arms across his chest as he looked down at me. You could almost see the suit threads straining against his biceps. He and I shared a similar build, which made it comical to me that he seemed to be trying to use his size to intimidate.

Lay his ass out.

"Big guy like you, protecting your smaller partner from a skinny meth head with no weapon all hopped up on shit. I can see that. That first shot probably would have put him out."

I stared at him.

140

"But it sounded to me like someone was trying to teach him a lesson, Bobbie." Carter squinted as he eyeballed me. "So, you either hit him like a semi splatters a deer on I-94, or you just kept swinging."

"What are you trying to say?"

He shrugged, shifting his position.

"Just saying, seems a bit overdone." We stared at each other long and hard, searching each other's eyes.

I wanted to murder his ass right now.

Fucking do it!

He broke the silence and took his eyes off mine, knocking a few times on the desk.

"Your boss said you had a rough call last night. He was gonna send you home."

I just stared at him. A sound was rising in my head – like metal groaning and straining under too much weight. It was mixed with a ringing in my ears.

"Carter, that's enough for now." Nick started to rise from his seat.

"That have something to do with your daughter?"

I exploded from my seat and wrapped my fists into the fabric of his coat, pushing him back down onto the desk. I drew back to swing and felt Nick wrap himself around me, locking my arm back and dragging me off the guy.

"Bobbie!" He pulled me back. "Calm down!"

I jerked out of Nick's grip and pointed a finger at Carter. "Don't fucking talk about my daughter. You don't know shit about me!"

141

Carter smoothed his coat and remained amazingly calm. In fact, the fucker was even grinning a little.

"I'll know a lot more soon." He stepped toward me, standing toe to toe, looking me dead in the eyes. "You're free to roam for now, specifically on Nick's good graces, but I just want you to know you're in my world now."

I felt legitimate fear at the statement. At the idea that anyone would consider me capable of murder. That I would be a suspect.

"I'm the guy they bring in to catch the ones who think they're invulnerable," Carter said, still staring at me. Looking good and deep. He was close enough that I could smell the wintergreen on his breath. "I always get 'em, because they make mistakes."

I stared back.

"They always make mistakes." He stepped back and rebuttoned his suit coat. "Every so often, someone gets stupid and makes my job easy. I like that you're leaning that way."

Nick had positioned himself somewhat between us, ready to split us if I jumped again. I looked to Nick then back to Carter.

"Don't go far, Bobbie." Carter grinned and put his glasses back on, stepping out of the office. Nick lagged a bit but was following him out. He looked at me from the doorway and shook his head.

"That was fucking stupid, B." He looked up and sighed, then back to me. "You're gonna want to answer the phone when I call you later. We're waiting for some security footage from the restaurant. What am I gonna see on that tape Bobbie?"

"Nothing, Nick. Fuck! Cindy and I just talked about Sarah after I walked her to her car."

Nick nodded and seemed to let his body slump a bit.

"Then that's what I'll be looking for, buddy." He shut the office door as he left, leaving me to sit in the empty office.

The air was heavy, suddenly stuffy and making it difficult to breathe. All I wanted in that moment was Holly.

My thoughts went to Cindy and I looked down, staring at my hands in my lap. They weren't trembling anymore. I studied my palms and my fingers. How many times had I dragged people back from the brink? It was ludicrous that anyone would think I was capable of this.

I turned my hands over, looking at the swollen and bruised knuckles.

"Shit."

*****

I walked in long, determined strides across the garage, heading for the back lot. It was the last spot I had checked for Hunter and the truck. The whole sit down didn't take long, but I imagine Britski had him washing the tires with a fucking toothbrush or something.

143

All I wanted to do was get out of the building. Get myself back on the road, lose myself in work, and try to process this shit later.

I kept checking my phone, as if Nick were going to call so soon. They had just left.

The anger that had been resting like a flow of lava in me had mostly been replaced now. Fear, paranoia, and sorrow at the loss of two people that I cared about deeply.

I swallowed it.

The ground level garage was a flurry of activity. It always was. Crews returning to decon and clean vehicles, others getting ready to roll out on shift. I normally would have had to wade through a handful of conversations walking through.

My fast pace and scowl likely flagged me as "do not fuck with."

I caught some glances and a wave or two, but no one tried to interact beyond that.

Pushing through the large steel door at the rear of the garage, I squinted under the bright sunlight that was a stark contrast of the garage lit poorly by halogens. My eyes adjusted and I scanned the lot for Hunter.

The rig was up against the high fence of the lot, backed in. Hunter was leaning on the hood of the ambulance nearly face to face with Sara. I watched them a moment before I started to move.

They were laughing, and their posture couldn't be more open with one another. As I drew closer, Hunter raised a hand and touched her chin. She looked up to him and they didn't waste any time falling into a soft kiss.

144

I actually stopped and stared. I had never, in the entirety of time, seen that guy kiss a woman like that.

I've seen crushing embraces, gropes, grabs, slaps, and spanks. I've even shared a woman with him in the past. From personal experience, Hunter is not a sensual individual.

Smooth as fuck, but not sensual.

For Hunter to kiss her like that meant something.

I continued walking again, and they continued to kiss. Long, soft, and very not-Hunter-like. They broke off the embrace as I stepped up, coughing. She looked a bit embarrassed and her cheeks flushed – though I'm not sure if it was from being caught in the act, or if it was the kiss.

Hunter grinned at me and leaned back against the front of the ambulance.

"Hey brother." His grin faded a little as he studied my face and he squinted. "You hear anything about Lily?"

"It's a long story. We'll talk in the car. I just want to get back in service, Logan."

"Ok, boo." He threw the keys to me. I caught them and stared before shaking my head, throwing them back. "No man, I don't want to drive right now."

Hunter caught the keys and nodded, looking to Sara and winking. "You can sit in my lap while I drive if you want."

She slapped his shoulder and turned to head for the side door of the ambulance.

"Oh, fuck me, what does he want now." Hunter looked past me and I turned, spotting Britski walking toward us. "That motherfucker made me mop the bathroom. And not the good one either. The shitter in the garage. Filthy fucks in there, man."

Britski walked right by us and stopped Sara before she got in the truck.

"I need you to head in and grab an incident form from Ella in HR before you go back out." Britski gave me a sideways glance as he stepped aside, gesturing for her to start moving. "I want it by end of shift."

She nodded and settled into a jog. We all watched her go, Hunter most attentive to her parting bounce. When she had covered a good distance, Britski stepped up and gave me a flat look.

"I understand what you've gone through, and I recognize that it's not always easy." He was speaking calmly, in a tone that I can't recall him ever using. "But I can't let you go back on the road unless you can convince me without a doubt that you're not a loose cannon about to lose your shit on the next person who looks at you sideways."

My gaze settled to the ground and I nodded before looking to Hunter. He was just watching me. I knew he was concerned about all the shit, and how I had been acting. I was concerned, too.

Today was a clusterfuck.

I honestly didn't know if I was good or not. How the hell could I promise something if I didn't even know if I was alright?

One thing was certain, I had no intention of sitting at home in my empty house, stuck in my head, until shit got resolved. The only place that was going to help me get through this was the road.

"I'm good, boss."

Britski's eyebrows went up and he laughed.

"Shit, I kind of like you this way. You're not such a fucking smartass."

"I'll make up for it next time." I smirked. He clapped my shoulder and nodded at me.

"No more Mike Tyson shit. Don't make me regret letting you stay on. I know you hate my wormy fucking guts, Badger, but I still care about my own and look out for you guys."

"Relax, Cap'. I'll keep an eye on him."

"Yeah, 'cause that makes me feel better." He shook his head and walked away, shouting back to us, "Get back on the road, there's calls stacking up and dispatch is having a goddamn fit."

We both watched him walk away before I turned to Hunter, pursing my lips. I didn't want to say it.

"Lily's dead. Cindy was found dead, too."

Hunter stood up from leaning against the hood of the rig, his head doing a double take. "What?!"

"I don't know. Cindy, I guess sometime after we left the restaurant. Lily was in the hospital already, so…" I trailed off.

Hunter's hands went to his forehead, rubbing slowly back over the stubble of his scalp.

"Holy shit, Bobbie. Why the fuck would someone kill Cindy?" He was shaking his head incredulously. "I mean, she was a mean fucking cunt but she was great. What the shit, Bobbie?!"

"The fucking detective thinks I did it."

"Who, Farzo? Man, fuck that guy." I put my hand up to stop him, shaking my head.

"No. No, the other guy. Farzo doesn't think it was me. This other asshole, Carter. Drilled me about the call last night and brought up the fight with that meth head."

"What call, the gun shot girl at the casino? What's that got to do with Cindy?" Hunter looked as confused as me.

"Who knows. He brought up Sarah, too." I rubbed my forehead. "I fucking jumped on him."

"You hit a cop?" Hunter's eyes went wide and he started laughing.

"No, no I just… grabbed him. I lost my shit. I look like a fucking lunatic."

Hunter put a hand on either of my biceps, giving them a squeeze as he stepped up to me. He looked up at me with a toothy grin.

"I got you, boo. We just need to get through today, get you some sleep, and this will all clear. We both know you didn't hurt anyone."

I nodded in agreement.

"I mean, you did just beat that guy's ass fucking silly. But we both know you're too much of a fucking pussy to do anything but slap around meth heads."

I laughed a bit and shoved him off me, heading for the passenger side. "Get in the truck, you dickhead."

We held in the lot waiting for Sara to come back out. I looked to Hunter sitting in the driver's seat, his eyes distracted as he stared at the building. Like he was wishing and waiting with baited breath for her to come out that steel door.

"That was a pretty serious kiss."

He looked at me and grinned, nodding in agreement.

"I like her. I like this one a lot." He shifted in his seat and took a deep breath, turning to lean his elbow on the steering wheel as he looked at me. His face was suddenly lit like a teenager experiencing their first crush. "She's smart, brother. She makes me want to be chill, too. I like that."

If there was one thing to come from this shitty fucking day, it was that. I had been waiting for him to look at a woman like that for years. That was the same way I used to look when I thought about Holly.

Still do, really.

Sometimes.

Sara appeared out of the steel door of the garage, breaking into a jog across the lot toward the truck. Her assets had a great bounce, and I could appreciate that she was more than just curves and flesh. She definitely had a decent head on her shoulders.

"I'm gonna name our first kid Bobbie." He slapped my arm as he watched her run.

"What if it's a girl?" I pulled a cigarette out from the pack in my breast pocket and lit it in the truck. Not something I'd normally ever do, but today seemed like a day of firsts.

"Nonsense." He slapped the dashboard. "This cock only shoots little boys."

I just stared at him with my brow furrowed, half grinning around my cigarette

"Ugh… Shut the fuck up." He turned to start the rig, fastening his belt as Sara opened the side door and hopped into the back.

*****

You couldn't go too long working one of the Downriver posts without eventually catching a basic call. Mid-afternoon the hospital staff tries to dump patients and clear beds. The BLS rigs get overwhelmed so they'll pull a few available ALS trucks to move patients to nursing and rehab facilities.

They weren't bad calls. They were easy, minimal work, chat with the patient and you're done in about twenty. It was when you got stuck in the transfer loop that it started to wear on you.

We'd heard from other crews that it was looking like one of those days, and we got pushed right into the loop out of Oakhill Main.

Any other day I'd grumble, but I was happy to take simple calls today.

Simple I could handle. Normal felt good.

150

Hunter didn't complain. Not a single peep about taking a BLS transfer. He was enamored with Sara and continued to chat with her through the pass through as he drove.

Glancing out the window, I watched the painted lines slice by as he pushed us along in the fast lane of I-94. I propped my face in my hand, waiting impatiently for my phone to ring; the call back from Nick.

I knew what the tape would show. I knew what the call would be. But I needed it to come from him to feel fully validated. That phone call would break the chains keeping me bound to an insurmountable level of anxiety.

Pushing it down was difficult.

Hunter was right. I just needed to get through the shift.

I really needed that fucking phone call.

Hunter was pushing the rig well over the speed limit in the fast lane, consistently passing and weaving around cars. There was no reason to rush, really, but he always said when you can legally break the speed limit you might as well enjoy it.

He preferred to run at about 85 mph, just enough to pass pretty much everyone.

Which is why I was surprised when a large pickup was rolling up on our passenger side, slowly trying to overtake us in the center lane.

"What the fuck is this guy doin'?"

"What?" Hunter stopped his conversation with Sara and leaned forward, glancing over at my window as I pointed at the truck that was running even with us. It was one of those extended cab super duty trucks, built for heavy loads and industrial work.

Except they were also the truck of choice for a lot of urban cowboys that never hauled anything heavier than a cooler full of shitty beer.

Hunter laughed as the jet black pickup truck surged ahead. "That's job security right there. We'll have to scrape his guts off the road later on tonight, watch."

The truck must have been going at least 95 mph as it rolled a few car lengths ahead of us.

Then it suddenly swerved into our lane and locked up its brakes. I briefly saw smoke curl from its tires as we came up on it fast.

Hunter cursed and tried to slow the rig but he knew there wasn't enough room. Yanking the wheel, the ambulance leaned hard as he moved to the shoulder.

He lost control of the rig.

There was the brief sound of crossing rumble strips, following by a thunderous F-bomb from Hunter before the front of the rig hit the start of the cement K-rails. The rig jumped.

I was grabbing the handle over my door, my other hand against the dashboard as the windshield filled with nothing but blue sky.

I don't know how long the truck was airborne.

It felt like eternity, the sound of the diesel engine racing without the friction of the ground to keep the wheels from spinning free.

Gravity seemed to shift as the truck tipped in the air.

The ground was coming at me in the side window, then glass exploded. My head was rocked against the frame of the truck and I nearly blacked out.

All I could hear was the sound of metal being shredded as the truck slid on its side. Sara was screaming in the back. I had my arm pressed against the ceiling, holding me up as the ground slid by just outside the passenger window.

Dirt and rocks were spitting up at me, pelting me in the face and arms.

The truck finally slid to a stop.

Through the fractured and battered windshield I could see that we had come to a stop on our side, stretched across a couple lanes in the freeway.

It didn't last long. I heard the sound of tires screeching and the truck was rocked by a massive hit again, sending us spinning and sliding. Not as far this time, and not as long.

"SHIT!" Hunter shouted. "MOTHERFUCKER!"

"Sara! Are you okay?!" I shouted, somewhat turned in my seat, but I couldn't look back. I was still belted in and the belt was locked, giving me no slack.

There was no response.

I feared the worst. She wasn't belted in and had been propped in the pass through to the cab so she could shoot the shit with Hunter.

"Sara!" Hunter shouted and struggled to get his belt free. He briefly fought the strap before pulling his knife from his belt. I coughed as I smelled burning electrical and exhaust. Something was starting to burn, the acrid smell filling the cab.

Hunter used the seat belt cutter on the handle of his knife to rip himself free of the belt, dropping down on top of me. I cursed and tried to help him keep his footing as he cut my belt free.

He rose and looked over me, through the pass through.

"Oh God."

"Is she hurt?" It was a stupid question. His words sounded like he had been gutted. In all the shit we've seen together, I'd never heard those words from him. Not like that.

I braced against the dash and frame, standing to look into the back.

There wasn't much left of the back.

It was nearly collapsed, and light was shining in from the split box of the ambulance.

There are no words to describe what the body looks like when it's been thrown about in a high-speed accident, and then crushed by the impact of another vehicle hitting a stationary object.

But it didn't look like Sara anymore.

We both stood there shocked before we heard tires screech again. Another impact, but not as significant as the last. The ambulance rocked.

Another screech of tires.

Another collision shook us.

The sounds and vibrations continued, and I knew vehicles were piling up.

"Get out. Now." I shoved Hunter and pointed up.

I boosted him up, steadying his balance as he scrambled up and out of the driver's side door. Following suit, Hunter helped pull me up and onto the truck. There was smoke rolling from the underside of our rig.

Looking back, we could see a row of vehicles that had been caught in the chain reaction. At least a dozen passenger vehicles. The first one that hit us was a minivan, like mine, and it had thoroughly buried its front end in the box of our ambulance.

If the violent landing didn't kill Sara, that collision did it.

Flames jumped from the front of the van buried in the rig. We could hear a woman screaming from inside.

Hunter jumped from the truck immediately, and I followed behind. The van was on an angle with the driver's side buried but the passenger side was mostly exposed – though rather crushed.

Hunter was peering through the smoke, calling out to the woman in the driver's seat. She slowly started to crawl across, coughing and struggling to breathe through the smoke. Dragging her through the window, we supported her weight and carried her together away from the truck to a few lanes away.

I looked back down the row of wrecked vehicles. They were all bad, but not as bad as hers. Some sat motionless in the wreck, others were bloodied and climbing out of their mangled cars. Traffic across all lanes was at a dead stop.

155

"My daughter," the woman choked out barely audible words. She coughed hard and gagged on the smoke she had inhaled, then repeated it.

Hunter and I both looked at each other, then back to the minivan. The underside was now burning and the front end was nearly engulfed. The flames were starting to climb the sides.

He didn't even hesitate.

I watched Hunter bolt toward the van. He slowed and staggered as he got close enough to feel the heat from the growing flames.

"Hunter! STOP!"

He didn't hear me, or didn't care to stop. Despite the heat that even I could feel starting to peel off the wreck, he stepped right into the flames and yanked the side door of the van open. I heard him growling and yelling as he reached in, working despite the flames that were rolling up all around him.

Hunter was standing directly in the fire.

He couldn't have been in it more than a few seconds when he fell backward clutching a child to his chest.

Hunter staggered and ran back toward me, stumbling several times. As he got closer I could clearly see the extent of his injuries. He dropped next to me, setting the child down She was burned, but not nearly as bad as he.

The mother clutched at her daughter, tears flowing, as Hunter fell over and rolled to his back, gasping and squeezing his eyes shut.

His uniform was charred heavily and smoking, especially his pants. Any exposed skin was deeply burned.

There was nothing I could do for him.

The little girl was awake, crying loudly. I couldn't treat her burns.

The mother likely had a serious injury given the amount of blood I could see on her clothes.

Grabbing the portable from my belt I did the only thing I could do.

"Dispatch... Alpha 611... involved in a multi-vehicle collision... on I-94 near Southfield. Need Fire, ALS, and PD." My voice was shaky as I looked around, my eyes going to Hunter. "Ten.. fourteen.. maybe cars. Mass casualty incident... my partner is down. Repeat, medic down!"

Dispatch confirmed immediately.

Hunter was unconscious, and I was completely helpless.

I tried to get up to move to him, to do what I could. My head throbbed and the ground spun up from beneath my feet. I caught myself with my hands and vomited onto the pavement.

The burning vehicles were heating the chill spring wind, blowing hot air and smoke across the expressway, enveloping us. I gasped after retching, sucking in a lungful. Gagging and choking on the air I threw up harder, dry heaving with my face close to the pavement.

My head was pounding already. The strain of vomiting intensified it and made my vision blur.

I dropped the radio and fell over near my partner, squinting over Hunter as the ambulance burned on the other side of the expressway with Sara's body inside.

There was no sign of the truck that had run us off the road.

The radio crackled near me.

"Alpha 611, multiple units are rolling. Stay with us."

The sounds of the woman and her daughter crying were growing distant and hollow, replaced by a familiar ringing. Darkness crept at the edge of my vision as I lay my head back on the hot asphalt.

My chest burned. My head throbbed.

"Alpha 611, copy last traffic?"

I blinked slowly and closed my eyes.

"611, copy? What is your status?"

Chapter 7 – Descent

The first thing I notice in the morning when I wake up is how my mouth always tastes like an ashtray. That's quickly remedied with another cigarette to freshen it up.

I rolled my tongue around in my mouth. It was dry, tacky, and my lips were sticking to my gums.

My mouth tasted like peroxide.

My eyes felt heavy and impossible to open. I exhaled and started to move, groaning quietly. Everything hurt.

I could barely lift my hands. It felt like all I could do was shift my fingers a bit.

Swallowing hard, I could feel the dryness extending down my throat.

What felt like a rolling cough only came out as a quiet, pathetic wheeze.

"Bobbie? Oh, my God, Bobbie?!"

Holly.

Her hands closed on my hand. I tried to speak but couldn't seem to make any sound other than grunting.

She shushed me quietly and gripped my hand tighter. "It's ok, baby. Just relax. Relax, you're alright. I'm here."

Wherever here was.

I turned my head slowly toward her voice, feeling the tug of plastic on my face. A nasal cannula. I was suddenly aware of the steady flow of oxygen blowing into my nostrils from the tubing.

Aware of the bent position in which I was laying, like a recliner.

Hospital?

Why?

I tried to open my eyes again. One of them cooperated, opening just a slit.

My eyes were assaulted by the light and I squeezed them tight again.

"Bobbie, it's okay. Don't try to do too much." I felt her soft fingers run down the side of my face. They were cold, almost like ice, but they flooded me with warmth.

I opened my eyes again, both this time. A little more.

Holly looked at me, bathed in a fluorescent halo of light, and she smiled through watery eyes.

I sniffled at her.

She lost herself somewhere in a mix of laughter and crying, her hand cupping my face, the other squeezing my hand tightly. "Hi baby," her voice cracked through the tears.

"Hey." I managed to speak, letting the word ride out on an exhale of breath.

She let out another mingled chirp of crying and laughter before releasing my hand. I heard a tone go off over my head as a voice came over loudly into the room.

"Nurses station, can I help you?"

So, a hospital then.

160

"My husband is awake!" Holly proclaimed loudly, her fingers stroking my face. Her touch was so soothing, her voice more comforting than I think I ever recall feeling.

Her reaction is what concerned me.

I tried to take in the room around me, letting my head roll to the other side as I blinked slowly. My vision was still fairly blurry. Even Holly's face wasn't completely clear.

It still felt like I had weight strapped all over my body, and I was starting to notice a dull throb in my head. I scowled at the discomfort.

"What's wrong, Bobbie?" Her hand closed on mine again.

I tried to say 'water', but nothing came out. I just mouthed the words, I think.

Holly shushed me again.

"Hold on, Bobbie. The nurse is coming."

There wasn't enough in the whole of my body to feel frustrated… or feel anything for that matter. I just felt relaxed save for the mild throbbing in my head. I just lay there, content with waiting.

Maybe less about being content. I didn't really have a choice.

Sleep was coming back to me. It felt warm and inviting.

*****

Sharp pains in my foot jerked me awake and I yanked my foot upward, bending my knee. Blinking under the fluorescent lights I scowled around me. There was still some blur in my vision but it was mostly gone.

Holly was standing next to me, and smiled at me. There were others in the room... a nurse and a doctor maybe.

"Sorry about startling you, Bobbie," the man spoke. "I just needed to make sure you were with us."

He slid a small pen into his white coat, offering me a tight, professional smile. He looked young for a doctor, but then it wouldn't be the first time I met residents and physicians younger than myself.

Settling back into the bed I sighed and nodded. My throat was still dry and parched. I made the motion for a drink.

"Oh, of course. Ah..." The doctor paused. "Ice chips for now, just to make sure you can swallow alright. You were intubated for a while."

I waved him off and nodded. The nurse slipped out as the doctor gestured at her before turning back to me.

"We're going to run through some questions Bobbie, to check your mental state. I'm sure you're familiar with the process."

I nodded and watched him flip through some charted notes as he stood at the foot of the bed. He kept his eyes on the paper as he slowly walked around to my bedside. He proceeded to run through a number of tests, checking my pupils with a small light before moving over to examine the side of my head.

162

"Everything looks good, vitals are solid." He looked to the nurse as she returned with a large foam cup full of small ice chips. I wasted no time in dumping a mouthful in, crunching thirstily and exhaling through my nose.

God the ice was so good. It hit me with that familiar feeling of satisfaction, like what comes from slamming an ice-cold Coke in the middle of summer when it's roasting balls outside.

I shut my eyes and chewed the ice, letting it melt as I settled my head back into the pillow. The relief to my dry mouth and throat was instantaneous. I finished three more mouthfuls while they all waited patiently around me.

"Oh God…" I was able to croak out in a somewhat raspy voice, though much clearer.

The doctor smiled and rested his clipboard on the side rail, propping his hands on it as they overlapped.

"Can you tell me your name?"

"Bobbie Badger." I squinted at him, trying to get my eyes to focus better.

"Good. Do you know where you're at?"

"Hospital." I looked around again. The room was familiar but I couldn't place which hospital. I knew it was in the Oakhill system. Their rooms all looked the same. "Oakhill Center somewhere."

"That's right. Oakhill Main." He tapped his fingers on the clipboard. "What about the year?"

"2017," I replied without missing a beat.

He nodded with satisfaction, lifting the clipboard to scribble some notes.

"That's good, Bobbie." Holly squeezed my hand while he spoke. "You're recovering from the concussion pretty well given the blow you took to the head."

The whole accident started flooding back on me, but I ignored most of it. My mind locked on to Hunter and I looked to the doctor, then to Holly.

"Where's Hunter?"

The doctor looked to her and her grip on my hand tightened.

"Bobbie…"

"I'll be out in the hall." The doctor stepped back before retreating from the room and closing the door behind him.

"Holly… where's Hunter?"

Her eyes welled up and she put a hand over her mouth, taking a deep breath. She took a second to calm herself before looking me in the eyes.

"Hunter's in intensive care, Bobbie. He has second and third degree burns over a lot of his body." She held my hand, staring into my eyes. Her lip quivered. "They said the burns are internal, too. In his airway. They don't know if he'll make it, baby."

I closed my eyes and felt that hollow, familiar rage rising again. Why did he have to go running back into that shit…

"He did what Hunter does, Bobbie." She knew exactly what I was thinking.

And she was right, but that didn't make it any easier to accept what she was saying.

It was just too much.

"I want to see him."

164

"Bobbie, honey you-"

"I want to see him!"

I interrupted her, shouting hoarsely. The effort strained my throat and stung deep.

Holly flinched.

That was something I'd never seen her do. Ever. Not with me. Not with anyone.

"Okay, Bobbie."

*****

Hunter was in an isolation pod in the ICU. I couldn't get access to him directly, not like I wanted. With the nature of his burns he had to be isolated to minimize infection. They had him ventilated, sedated, and completely covered in dressings. I watched the monitor in his room through the glass, staring at the steady rhythm of the heart monitor.

His chest was rising and falling in a precise rhythm, but not by his own control.

The vent was doing all the breathing for him.

I sat in the wheelchair in the hall; my eyes went to my own hands and to the IV in the back of my right hand. A heavy sigh escaped me, and I felt Holly's hands on my shoulders. I reached up and touched her, rubbing my fingers along her own.

I was thankful for her in that moment, but the idea of her only increased the pain I felt inside.

Not that I was angry with her. Not right now.

165

It was the sharp realization that Hunter didn't have anyone. Short of the other crews we knew well, Hunter had no family. No one that could come and sit with him, talk to him, or mourn him.

The only woman I had ever seen him legitimately fawn over was dead before his own eyes. However brief he felt that crushing weight, I knew it all too well, and I knew what it felt like.

I also knew what to do with it.

I pushed that pain down and swallowed it.

"How long…" I turned my head slightly toward Holly's hand that I was touching. "How long was I out?"

"It's been four days, Bobbie. They were worried you weren't going to wake up. The swelling was bad. They had to relieve the pressure…"

Holly trailed off and squeezed my shoulder.

"I'm just glad you're okay, baby." She bent over and wrapped her arms around me from behind. I could feel her familiar strength. She didn't look it, but Holly was incredibly strong compliments of her military training and consistent weight training for the department.

I felt her breath on the side of my neck as she squeezed me tighter. Her scent filled my nostrils and it was a beautiful – though brief – distraction from everything I was attempting to process.

Four. Fucking. Days.

A lot can happen in four days. You could lose your best friend.

"He's not gonna make it, is he?" I stared back at Hunter's motionless body in the isolation pod. Holly tightened her arms for a second, hugging me.

"I don't know, Bobbie."

"He's such an asshole. Stupid fucking trauma trooper."

"Bobbie, don't talk like that."

"He'd still be here, and be fine, if he hadn't run back to that fucking car." I clenched my teeth, staring at him.

I'd throttle him until he woke if I could get away with it. And that's just so he would be awake when I slapped the shit out of him.

Holly stood and walked around me, never letting a hand leave me. She squatted down and my eyes moved to her face. Cheeks wet with recent tears, eyes swollen and tired. She looked absolutely exhausted.

I remember that face well. I'd seen it a lot over the years when we would try to stay awake after working doubles, just to spend a little more time together.

It was also how she looked through much of the pregnancy, during childbirth, and all the countless hours spent awake being a mother to our beautiful Sarah. I just stared at her, gazing into her eyes. A sadness crept over me and tried to escape.

Holly noticed and grabbed both my hands in hers as she crouched in front of me.

She looked so beautiful out of uniform, even if she was just wearing a tattered pair of jeans and a U of M hoodie.

Goddamn beautiful.

"We need to get you back to your room."

167

"Just a few more minutes."

*****

I was supposed to be on fairly strict bedrest for the observation period, but I don't listen too well. Most of my recovery time was spent in a wheelchair outside of Hunter's isolation pod. If Holly wasn't available to push me there, then I was rolling myself.

More than one nurse had scolded me about taking off on my own without notifying them, and I'd been retrieved twice by the staff to be taken back to my room after spending too long.

There was no such thing as "too long" as far as I was concerned.

If Hunter woke up, then I wanted to be there for it.

By halfway through my second day I was ready to walk out. In fact, I had tried. Despite being unsteady on my feet I was in the process of getting dressed when Holly came in.

My plan was to be ready to walk when she came back in.

I got as far as a standing there in my boxer briefs, having just removed the IV catheter myself along with my gown. She stopped fast as she opened the door.

My pants were in my hands and I waved at her.

"Get back in bed, Bobbie."

"Nope." I started to put my pants on and tipped a little due to a slight spell of vertigo. I caught the bed rail to steady myself and tried to make it look natural.

Holly came toward me with determined steps, scowling.

168

"Bobbie Badger, get back in bed… now." She was giving me that look. Her eyes were cutting through me as I looked at her. I had my pants halfway up one leg when I paused.

I started to pull them up the rest of the way.

"If your other foot slides into those pants, I'm going to sign a petition to have you placed under psych evaluation with a 72-hour hold."

She stepped closer and was looking me dead in the eyes, despite her short stature. Easy to do since I was hunched still.

"No you won't." I stood and let my pants fall.

"Try me."

I sighed and sat back on the bed, rubbing my hands across my face.

"I can't be here another day, Holly. I'm going out of my mind." My hands fell, shoulders slumping and I sat there feeling defeated. All I could think about, all day long, were the people who lost their lives. Not just my Sarah, but Lily and Cindy… and our 3rd rider.

Now Hunter was probably on his way to checking out.

People with significant burns like his don't have a good chance of recovery. Infections set in within a few days and everything starts shutting down from sepsis. It's a fucking terrible way to go – but at least he wouldn't be awake.

He'd been with me for six years. Just six years of my career, but I can't remember what things were like before Hunter.

I don't even want to think about what it would have to be like without him.

Just a few stupid mistakes had claimed so many lives.

169

My own failure to act killed Sarah. Friends were murdered… and now this stupid accident.

I looked back up to Holly, realizing I had left her standing in silence as I got lost in thought with my eyes at the floor.

"I know you've got a lot on your mind, Bobbie. You've got to try not to get stuck in that. You know what it does."

She was talking about Grepps… and she was probably also referring to Jansen and Dias. All three of them took their own lives over a mix of personal shit and the load from this career. All three of them were long-term career medics.

Two of them were close friends and mentors.

All three were suicides.

I nodded, knowingly, my shoulders sagging a little more.

"I'll be alright. You can't blame me for wanting to leave. I spend every day working in these places. The last thing I want to do is sleep here."

"It ain't the Westin downtown, baby, but you've got me." She swung her hips a little as she walked to me, pressing her body to mine and wrapping her arms around my head. I rested the side of my face against her stomach and closed my eyes, my hands holding onto her hips.

I felt her fingers on the side of my head, touching the bandage gently that covered the wound site. The throbbing was gone, now it was just the occasional discomfort - especially when I changed positions too quickly.

Right now, Holly was the one thing that was keeping me sane. I held such adoration for her, and for devoting her time to being here with me.

170

There was no anger, loathing, or resentment right now. I don't know if it's buried, or gone permanently. I just know that I would stay wherever she wanted me to stay if it meant being able to bury my face in her like this and smell that lavender shea butter.

Her fingers played across my scalp, dragging against the growing stubble. My beard was getting thick as well. I just couldn't bring myself to shave. Or do much of anything.

Even the most mundane tasks seemed like an irritation and interruption – even though I wasn't doing anything else.

My hands squeezed her hips, and then squeezed again.

I loved the extra cushion she carried in her hips and ample ass. My hands slid around to slowly grab handfuls of her bottom.

She shifted and giggled, stepping back out of my pawing hands.

"Bobbie… behave." Her eyes widened as she looked at me. I could tell I had pushed the right buttons by how she was grinning at me. She wagged a finger and walked toward the bathroom. "You'll get that once you've learned to listen and behave."

My eyes studied her curves and I felt a little fire grow in me.

I hated seeing her go, but I liked to watch her leave.

"Yes ma'am." I grinned, watching her enter the bathroom and shut the door. I looked around the room and down to my hand, staring at it briefly before punching the nurse call button on the remote attached to the bed.

171

A beep came back from the speaker. "Nurses station, can I help you?"

"…My IV fell out again."

*****

"I'll go bring the car around, Bobbie." Holly slung a bag over her shoulder containing the personal things she had brought to the hospital for me. I sat on the bed as she left the room, dressed in my own clothing finally.

They had kept me under observation for a mind-numbing four days to closely monitor my condition. While I loathed it, I recognize that it was necessary. It wasn't until this morning I woke to find myself virtually symptom free with my balance almost completely restored.

There were still some lingering things, but the doc felt I was fine to head home.

Returning to work was apparently a no-go. At least not until I was medically cleared.

Not that I really wanted to go back without Hunter anyhow.

Hunter…

I sighed and rubbed my hands down my jeans. I felt selfish and a little ashamed for inwardly celebrating busting out of this place knowing he was still here. That there was no one to sit with him.

A heard a light tap at the door and looked up.

It was Blake.

I furrowed my brow and gave him a puzzled look. Genuine shock is what I felt. He had disappeared the same day Lily was killed, and I thought something may have happened to him. The thought had also crossed my mind that he might have killed his grandmother, but that seemed like a stretch for a fairly well-adjusted kid.

"Jesus, Blake." My posture straightened as he walked into the room, bobbing his head and giving me a slight smile.

"Hey…" He gave me a loose wave. "I heard about… what happened to you and your partner. I just wanted to see how you were doin."

I put my hands up, shrugging lightly.

"Going home, so not all bad. Hunter is still in ICU. Don't know about him." I watched Blake, sadness crossing his face.

"I remember Hunter, met him a couple times. He was nice. Sorry about that."

"It's okay, Blake. These things happen on the job sometimes. We know it every time we get in the rig."

"About the other morning…" He put his hands inside the pockets of his hoodie, shrugging a little.

A young guy strolled in with a wheelchair, head bobbing to some unheard rap track rolling around in his head. He pushed a wheelchair into the room and looked at me, giving me a silent nod indicating that he was ready to take me down.

"Time to go." I looked back to Blake. "Sorry to hear about your grandmother. My offer stands still. Come over sometime and visit. And don't worry about the other morning. I know how you feel. We'll work it out."

173

"Look forward to it." He turned to leave, pausing in the doorway. I stood and settled into the wheelchair to be carted down to the lobby like an invalid. Hospital policy – every patient leaves in a wheelchair or on a stretcher when discharged.

Stupid policy.

My eyes met Blake's as he lingered. He stared at me for a few seconds before speaking.

"I'll see you real soon."

*****

"Damn! Is that yo ride?" The orderly rolled me through the automatic doors into the patient drop off and pickup outside. Holly was leaning against the car and wiggled her fingers at me with a wry little smile.

"The girl or the car?"

He clapped his hands and laughed as he bent down, locking the wheels of the wheelchair so I could stand up.

"Sheet. You be blessed with either, bruh."

I chuckled and stood up, thankfully to be walking out of the place. Holly stepped away from the car, dangling keys at me.

"I pulled her out of storage. Figured it would be a nice surprise for you, something to lift your spirits a little."

She was right.

I looked at the gleaming metallic green paint and glossed finish of the Shelby GT 500 and my heart fluttered. My entire life I had dreamed about and wanted this car. I fantasized about it.

Unfortunately, it wasn't something you could afford on a medic's wages. Not with a six-figure price tag.

To our benefit, Holly and I had always been very close to Lily and her husband. We found out when he passed away that he had restored a 1967 Shelby GT 500 and had it stored away. They knew my love for it, and Lily didn't know what to do with it when he passed. She refused to sell it off to a stranger.

So, she gifted it to me.

Lily insisted, despite my absolute refusal. She also refused to let me give her money for it. She said it's what her husband would have wanted – for it to go to someone who understood his love for that car.

He even called her Eleanor.

I'll never be ashamed to admit that I stood in that storage lot and cried when Lily gave me the keys.

I've driven it a few times, enough to keep it maintained and running. Otherwise it stayed in storage, only really coming out for the Woodward Cruise. I loved the car but still hadn't gotten used to driving it.

The goddamn thing was a monster and had a lot of power under the hood.

Car guys liked to talk cubic inches and output and all that shit when we took it to the cruise, or car shows. Some of them would argue that the GT 500 wasn't really THAT fast. One guy told me he took one for a test drive once and was disappointed it only turned 15.0 at 95.

I had no idea what he was talking about. I wasn't much of a car guy, but I knew what love is and I loved everything about Eleanor.

Now I was standing there admiring both of my beautiful ladies. The first day we drove it off that storage lot, Holly told me I should rename her. Give her something fitting to personalize it.

It didn't take me long to decide. I called her Jill.

She was my first crush when I was a teenager. I never worked up the nerve to talk to her, but we used to look at each other a lot. She was beautiful, like a dream. A unicorn I never caught.

Holly teased me, but she told me it was perfect.

I took the keys and bounced them in my hand, smiling. It was a good distraction. I had already started to forget some things.

Not everything.

But a lot.

I stepped to the car and opened the passenger door winking at Holly. "Please take a seat, my love." I bowed with a flourish. She cooed and slid into the car, smiling at me with a bob of her eyebrows.

Walking around I opened the door and slid in, the leather interior squeaking underneath me as I adjusted myself

176

"It always makes you happy when you can climb inside Jill, huh?"

I paused as I was about to insert the key, looking sideways at her with a light roll of my eyes.

"How many times are you gonna make that joke?"

"At least a dozen more." She beamed at me. "Go ahead, Bobbie. Put it in. You know how to turn her on."

"Oh. My. God. I regret naming this car." I sighed and shook my head. I slid the key into the ignition and Holly moaned, mockingly. Turning the key, the engine turned over and thundered to life. The sound of the rumbling exhaust echoed under the canopy of the drop lane and I grinned a little, looking at Holly.

She bit her lip.

The moan was a tease, but I knew what the sound of this car did to her.

I tapped the gas lightly and the front end of the car moved under the torque, the engine roaring up briefly from idle.

"Where do you wanna go, beautiful? I'm off work and I've got a full tank." I looked her up and down as she lay back in the dark leather seats. So beautiful. She ran a hand up her stomach to her chest before brushing her fingers across her neck and cheek.

"Hmm… Take me somewhere we haven't been in a while. Surprise me."

"You want to go fuck at the Dentist?"

She scoffed and swatted at me.

"Hey Badger, you big stud."

"That's me, honey."

I love it when she went for the movie lines.

"Take me to bed or lose me forever."

"Show me the way home, honey."

I rolled forward out of the drop lane, having briefly put it out of my mind what I was leaving behind and mashed the gas as we left the hospital. A little high octane therapy to briefly fill an otherwise expanding void.

*****

Holly seemed happy. Genuinely happy.

I can't imagine the scare of getting a call that Hunter and I were involved in a bad wreck. But that's not how it played out for her.

During my recovery, she told me that she had been one of the first vehicles responding to the scene. Her and a State trooper worked to resuscitate Hunter as other units arrived. She had maintained her calm and was able to help Hunter despite me laying there unconscious.

I was proud of her for that.

As we sat at a red light I saw her look to me, and my gaze met hers. The wind came in lightly through the window blowing her little blonde curls around her face. We smiled at one another.

Nothing much needed to be said.

I was less happy though. I felt unease and anxiety starting to creep back in. My smile was smaller than it should have been in that moment.

178

"What's the matter, baby?" Her hand touched mine as it rested on the shifter.

I shrugged a little as the light changed, shifting gears and rolling forward with traffic.

"I'm just starting to feel bad about leaving Hunter there. He doesn't have anyone."

"He's got us, Bobbie."

"I know. I'm wrestling with going back and sitting with him. I think I should."

"Bobbie, you've been at that hospital for over a week. Hunter is in good hands."

I didn't respond, and felt some irritation grow in me.

"Not two days ago I had to threaten you to keep you from signing out AMA and walking out of that hospital." She turned in her seat, getting a little cross with me. "Now, you're upset that we're leaving?"

"I just think someone should be there when he wakes up."

"Someone will be there, Bobbie. The hospital staff. There's nothing you can do."

Those last words stung. I know she didn't intend them to, but they had teeth.

This whole situation…this clusterfuck… all because there was nothing I could do.

Still can't do. Can't go back to work. Still can't do it.

I pulled a cigarette from my pocket and started patting myself down for a lighter. It had been days since I'd had one and was suddenly craving the fix as my irritation rose.

"OH no. You are not smoking in this car!"

179

Holly snatched the cigarette out of my mouth and I scowled at her as she tossed it out the window.

"No don't... throw it... away! Goddammit, Holly."

"You can't seriously say you were gonna smoke inside her?"

She was right. I didn't want to admit it, but she was right.

"There's a Kroger up ahead, pull in."

"I don't need to stop to have a cigarette."

"I know you don't," she quipped at me. "But we need to stop and get some things for the house. You have like zero food to make any kind of dinner with. I'm hungry, and if you want a little Holly then you've gotta feed me."

"I haven't felt the need to cook in a while. Hard to cook for one person."

Holly's eyes turned to me as I watched the road ahead. She didn't say anything but I knew that one stung her a little bit.

Maybe a lot.

A little bit of familiar anger rose up as I remembered coming home to find her things gone. I didn't want that mood right now.

"How about a tube steak?" I tried to take the edge off the previous statement with a little humor, even though part of me meant it.

Holly scoffed and rolled her eyes before looking back at me.

"You are so the opposite of romantic, Prince Charming. You're lucky you're good looking."

"It's hard to be this sexy, but it's sexy to be this hard."

"Oh Lord, stop while you're ahead. You're drying me out and ruining the ride." I smirked and turned into the parking lot of the shopping center, finding an empty space toward the end of the lot away from other vehicles. I didn't want any dings from stray carts or locals who exit their vehicles by kicking doors open like Chuck Norris.

I opened the door and started to get out when Holly put a hand on my arm. I looked back to her, one leg out of the Shelby.

"Bobbie, I'm not naïve." She was looking at me with this mix of cold fire and love in her eyes. "I know things aren't perfect between us. We've got things to work out."

"I don't want to do this right now, Holly." I pulled away from her and started to get out of the car again.

"Bobbie, that hurt."

I sat there, with my back to her, and my shoulders slumped a little.

The peace brought by the distraction of the car only lasted until the engine was off.

"What do you want me to say, Holly?" I stood up and shut the door. She exited her side and looked at me from across the hood.

"I want you to say that you're sorry, Bobbie. I want to know that you understand that hurt."

I put my hands on the roof of the car and looked at her.
She was right.

"Okay." I nodded. "You didn't deserve that. I'm sorry." I didn't feel a lot of sincerity in my apology. She probably didn't either. I wanted to mean it, but I wasn't there yet.

She smiled a little and nodded. It was enough for now. She at least deserved to hear me say it.

We fell into pace together toward the store, and she slid her hand into mine, interlacing our fingers.

It had been years since we held hands. I think Sarah was ten… on a vacation. We were walking on the beach.

With the time away and the little spats, and now holding hands, it was like trying to navigate dating all over again. I hated it, but at the same time there was a familiarity to it with Holly that turned our time together into a little game of cat and mouse.

I think I was enjoying the bits of conflict.

How frustrating. I'm too old for this shit.

*****

"I really don't have a preference. Whatever you want to make." I leaned on the cart. We had already been in the store for almost an hour while she tried to stock up on food for the house. I was questioning whether we would even be able to get all the groceries into the car.

Now she was hung up on exactly what to make for dinner tonight. She was stepping through the meat section picking up and examining every single cut.

"I can make you a steak tonight, do you want strip?

"Holly, I'm not really hungry. I don't know. I'll eat whatever you make."

182

There was no balance to my mental state it seemed. Everything was a constant roller coaster, and there was no telling what would send my anger and frustration spiraling.

The only thing that was constant was that feeling of always sitting near the boiling point. I was even getting pissed at the people parking their carts sideways or walking too slow.

I fantasized about running them over with my cart, or bouncing cans of soup off their skulls.

Holly let her head roll slightly to the side and gave me a look.

"I'm sorry, Holly, I don't know what I want. Just pick something."

"I don't want to *just pick something*." She threw the pack of steaks down into the cooler section and put her hands on her hips. "I want to cook for my husband and want *you* to tell me what *you* want to eat."

She had raised her voice and I was very much aware of some of the other people in the meat section glancing our way. Feeling uncomfortable, embarrassed, and increasingly angry I grabbed a package of ground beef and tossed it into the cart.

"What am I gonna cook with that?"

"Meatloaf is fine, I'm good with that. Can we go now?"

"Bobbie…" She looked in the cart and then at me. "You *hate* meatloaf."

"No I don't. Your meatloaf is good."

"You make faces every time I cook it."

I closed my eyes and put my hands up. Grabbing the package of ground beef from the cart I put it back and walked past her. "I'll be in the car when you're done."

"Seriously, Bobbie?" She scoffed behind me as I walked away. "…I love you."

I waved back to her with a forced smile and kept going.

Such a dickhead.

I felt cruel for acting that way, but it just didn't seem to take long in her presence for that wound to reopen.

My mind was always stuck on her leaving. I couldn't get past that.

And it only aggravated me more that she was suddenly back and trying to play house.

I loved her. I loved that she was around.

But I didn't love that she was trying to move on so easily. It wasn't that easy for me.

It still isn't.

She seemed like she was trying too hard to save me right now, and maybe I didn't want to be saved.

Didn't I?

I felt a weird rush and churn in my stomach at the idea of just being let go. Not being saved.

Of not waking up after the wreck.

That felt kind of welcoming right now.

The thought was interrupted as I exited the store into the parking lot. I checked the lane in front of the doors as I started to cross and came to a halt immediately.

There was a massive black truck sitting at the curb a few car lengths down. The windows were heavily tinted and it was sitting on lifted wheels. It was idling loudly, belching out a slow repetitive thud from its large exhaust. There was a shiny chrome Ford emblem in the middle of the black grill. The entire thing looked like it was made of carbon fiber or something, with sharp lines like a swat truck or the fucking bat mobile.

It looked exactly like the truck that ran us off the road. I stood there staring at it a moment. If there was anyone inside, I couldn't see them. The windows were flat black and swallowing any light that tried to bleed through.

There's no way it was the same truck.

There had to be hundreds, if not thousands, of black Ford pickups just like that scattered around the Metro Detroit area. I shook my head.

Don't be paranoid.

Still, I really wanted to walk up and knock on the window. But I didn't.

I continued walking and fished in my pocket for my keys.

The truck started rolling slowly.

I paused, assuming I'd give them room to go. The truck stopped as well.

"Really, guy? Jesus Christ…"

I gestured for them to go ahead but the truck didn't move. It just sat idling.

"Whatever." I shook my head and started walking again.

The engine of the truck surged loudly as it came rocketing away from the curb, straight at me. I froze for a moment before taking a few large strides and jumping out of the way.

That son of a bitch tried to run me down.

There was no doubt in my mind it was the same truck, for whatever reason, which means it was no accident.

The truck continued to roar through the parking lot, taking off between a row of cars and heading toward the exit. It had no license plate on the back.

"No you don't you motherfucker."

I sprinted as fast as my legs would carry me across the lot to my car. My head was pounding at the surge of adrenaline as I unlocked it and dove in.

Mashing the pedal, I left a trail of smoke as the Shelby roared forward. I couldn't see the truck anymore but I knew which way he left. It took only seconds to get into traffic. I nearly clipped a UPS truck as I exploded from the parking lot, oversteering and fishtailing as the rear end of the Shelby slid into the lane next to me.

A good two blocks or so ahead of me, I could see the truck weaving in traffic.

I gunned it to catch up, slipping quickly between the less exotic cars who were obeying the speed limit.

Unfortunately, I had the coordination of a drunk stock car rookie. I was all over the road, trying to keep the Shelby under control. If anyone were watching, it would have been the ugliest car chase ever seen.

When the driver realized I was behind them and gaining fast, they surged ahead. Whatever was under the hood of that truck wasn't a match for the sports car – even with my stupid ass behind the wheel.

The odometer was reading 70. Nearly double all the other cars going about their daily commute on the surface streets. They were blurs as we zipped between them.

My phone started ringing.

I pulled it from my pocket, weaving around another car to stay tight to the truck as I punched the answer button and put it on speaker.

"Hello?"

"Bobbie! Where ARE you? Did you leave me at the store?!"

I threw the phone into the passenger seat so I could focus on driving.

"Hi honey. Uh… yes."

"Well are you going to come back and get me? I'm standing in the parking lot with a cart full of fucking groceries."

I cussed as the truck took a hard corner into a subdivision. I jerked the wheel and the car fishtailed again, drifting into the corner and onto the subdivision street. The tires of the Shelby screeched around as I made the turn.

That was cool… like in a movie. Probably couldn't do it again if I wanted to.

"Bobbie, what was that? What are you doing?"

"I'm good!" I lied. "I'll be right there, honey. I just need to kill this asshole real quick."

I had intended to explain myself, but she was yelling through the phone. I tried to interrupt her when the truck came to a screeching halt in the middle of the residential street.

My brakes locked up as I ground to a halt, tires screeching again.

"…makes you think you can just leave me here?! Bobbie, what's going on?!" I could hear her much clearer now. I started to reply when the truck door opened. My whole body tensed and I didn't know what to do at that point.

An arm and part of a torso, along with a masked head leaned out.

They pointed a gun at me and I immediately dropped in my seat. The sound of gunshots rang out, hitting the car and windshield. Glass fell around me.

Déjà vu. Fuck!

"Bobbie! BOBBIE!" Holly's voice was filled with terror, screaming into the phone. I imagine she'd heard those shots plain as day.

I stayed as low as I could and threw the car into reverse, mashing the pedal and driving backwards down the street without looking. After a short distance, I stuck my head up to check behind me and spun the wheel.

The Shelby arced into a driveway, jumping the curb and sliding into someone's yard as I locked the brakes up. Shifting again, I stomped on the gas and the tires spit rocks, dirt, and grass at the house as I jumped the curb back into the street and sped off.

188

The windshield was fucked. I could see a few bullet holes in the hood. Checking my rearview, the truck was going the other way just as quickly.

"Fuck me… Holly, I'm coming back."

"Bobbie, what is going on. Talk to me!"

I fished the phone out of the passenger seat.

"Just sit tight, I'll be there in a minute. I'm fine." I hung the phone up so I could focus on the road, trying to see through a web of cracks and holes in the glass.

At least no one was dying in the back this time.

Chapter 8 - Catching Fire

What was supposed to be a quiet, semi-relaxing evening at home turned into several hours of dealing with police.

Not only did I have Holly chewing me a new ass, amongst concern for my safety, but the local PD were less than happy with the nature of the incident. I caught a serious lecture from more than one responding officer about the stupidity of my actions.

I think the only reason I didn't catch more shit was because Holly's county and she knew the officers on scene. Apparently being a victim of attempted murder is downplayed when you take a sport car on a car chase that ends in gunplay in a subdivision.

And tearing up someone's yard.

I was leaning against the front quarter panel of the Shelby with my arms crossed as Holly finished talking to the officers. She came walking back to me and was wearing her work face.

It was unusual to see her like that without her uniform and duty belt, all focused and serious. She stood in front o me, hands on her hips and looked me over. I quirked a brow and looked back at her.

Her hand came sharply across my face, stinging the skin. She didn't hit me anywhere near as hard as she usually does. It was enough to make me wince and for my head to throb a little. I looked back to her with one eye squeezed shut.

"Ow. Concussion?"

The salty, domineering look she was trying to give me melted away instantly and her eyes went wide. She cradled my face in her hands and started rubbing my cheeks before rubbing the sides of my head.

"Oh my God, Bobbie, I'm sorry. I wasn't thinking. I just.. wanted to change the mood. And I.. I thought." She was stumbling over her words and all her seriousness was gone. It was adorable, and I felt bad for her.

"It's fine, it's fine." I grabbed her hands to stop her from pawing at my face. "I'm alright. I just want to get home with you. Please."

I placed the keys in her hands.

"Maybe you should drive. I didn't do so hot last time."

*****

We caught a lot of strange looks on the way home. Most people around here weren't used to seeing a car like this just being driven around – even if we were in the heart of Ford country.

Add to it the bullet holes in the hood and windshield and we probably could have charged money for all the pictures that were being taken as people drove by. I could spot the gear heads easily by the looks of shock and head shakes.

191

Every once in a while, I got the Tommy Boy look from other drivers. You could see it in their eyes – that 'what'd you do?!' stare. All you can do in that situation is shrug, though I admit while sitting at a light I did catch the confused look of a guy riding a Harley after he looked over our front end.

I shrugged at him and then pointed at Holly. He looked at her in the driver's seat and started laughing.

"Don't do that."

"What?" I laughed at her. "It's not like you're not capable of it."

"What the fuck is that supposed to mean?" She scowled and looked at me, and I pointed at her face.

"Oh, shut the fuck up." She backhanded my chest as she drove. "You keep sassing me and see what happens when we get home."

"You're surprisingly violent to the victim of a car wreck that was just shot at." I prodded at her. "Shouldn't you be more caring and nurturing?"

Holly reached across and grabbed a handful of my crotch, squeezing right on the borderline of being too firm.

"You'll take whatever I decide to dish if you want my mouth."

Tingle.

"Yes ma'am."

Her hand moved from my growing bulge and she took my hand, locking her fingers in mine for just a moment. He eyes were smiling at me in a way that was bolder and more telling than her actual smile.

192

It was never any less refreshing when she looked at me like that, feeling her love pouring out of her. My eyes went back to the road as she drove, releasing my hand. I felt a bit empty as soon as she let go, but there was some warmth lingering from her touch.

She was trying hard to be here, with me, in the moment. Despite everything that happened. Despite the roller coaster ride of all the shit, she was still sitting next to me.

I struggled with resentment over her leaving, but I couldn't ignore how hard she was trying to be in the present.

Maybe it was time to let her.

Time to see if she was what was missing in order to heal fully.

She pulled us into the driveway at home. The sun was already creeping toward the end of the day and we sat in the car for a moment after she shut the engine off. Our heads turned to one another, meeting each other's gaze.

We just stared.

"Holly." My hand went to her thigh, stroking it softly and squeezing. "I know I haven't made it easy on you. I know you're trying. I haven't exactly made it easy on myself either."

I watched her as her eyes searched mine, trying to read me, to prepare herself for whatever I was going to hit her with.

"It's not easy to go back. I don't think we can go back."

I saw her eyes start to water and I leaned closer to her, taking her hand.

"But I want to try."

She started to cry, closing her eyes and putting a hand to her mouth.

"I spent those months without you. I know what it's like not to have you close. That's not a life I want to live anymore. I sure as fuck don't want to fill that void in my life with anyone else."

She squeezed my hand and wiped tears from her eyes, blinking and looking at me.

"Holly, I could never find anyone whose demons played well with mine. Not like yours. I don't know where you went when you left, but I know our bed is here. One of us has been sleeping in the wrong place."

Her face was a sea of emotion, swelling from somewhere deep. She didn't have any words because I think she was just overwhelmed. Any attempt to talk might just cause Niagara Falls to come surging forward.

"I want you to come back."

She laughed and cried at the same time, sniffling.

I sniffled back.

We sat in the waning light, under the darkening shade provided by the trees and houses around us. It was one of those moments they talk about – where you know you're with the right person when nothing has to be said at all, and the silence is comfortable.

"You're just sweet talking me because you want to fuck me again."

There's my Holly.

194

"Yes." I laughed softly. "Also, I'm terrified and I know you'll shoot any motherfucker that comes around because I clearly can't defend myself." I gestured to the windshield.

We locked eyes again.

"Jesus. You really know how to ruin like… the only romantic moment I've come up with in years," I said as I shook my head at her. She leaned over and put a hand to my face, running her thumb across the stubble as she placed her full lips to mine.

Her lips carried with them the lingering taste of salt from her tears. It was like the soft, perfect kiss we shared that morning before my shift.

Before all hell broke loose.

She broke the kiss and I could feel her hot breath on my face. I opened my eyes to see her gazing at me.

"Come inside, I'll make it up to you."

*****

Holly led me through the house, pulling me by the fingers as she walked backwards. She weaved her way expertly through the furniture, navigating turns without looking. She might have been gone for months, but this was her home for years and she knew it well.

We didn't rush to the bedroom. It was a slow walk, like a dance.

Nothing was said, no words were shared. We just watched each other. It felt like a honeymoon with the growing anticipation of what awaited.

I wanted to kiss her again, desperately.

She knew it, and she was keeping the pace deliberately slow to tease me.

I loved her fire, her sass, and her spirit. Holly could push just the right buttons, at just the right time, to make me submit. And I was happy to do so.

She is my queen.

I longed for every part of her body, but in that moment it was her lips that I craved most of all. It wasn't the taste, or the feel that made kissing her amazing.

It was the kiss exchanged thousands of times between our eyes before our lips even met.

She led me to our bedroom and pulled me toward the bed, turning and pressing me down gently by the shoulders. It didn't require any great deal of effort. I was absolute putty completely pliable and easy to mold.

Ready to submit.

I sat on the edge of the bed, looking up into her eyes. Her hands caressed the stubble of my cheeks, cradling my jaw and lifting my chin up a bit more.

"Take off your shirt, Bobbie."

I complied, quietly, pulling the t-shirt up and over my head. Before I could take it off fully I felt her grab and twist the fabric above and between my arms. Still caught up in the sleeves, with the shirt still covering the top of my face, froze. I couldn't see through the dark fabric.

196

Holly twisted the shirt tighter with one hand, binding my arms up. I didn't struggle, I didn't need to.

Didn't want to.

Through the fabric of the shirt I could smell her. The lavender and shea butter. She was close to me, and I parted my lips to sigh a little in anticipation.

Her lips touched mine, just brushing them at first. I leaned in hungrily and she pulled away from me.

"Slow, Bobbie."

I felt her lips again and I complied. I let her kiss me, only returning the touch of my lips… just barely. Her tongue grazed my lips before entering my mouth. Opening to her, I relaxed to let her dance her tongue around mine.

The heat rolled off her like a solar flare. I knew her body was close to me.

Holly's lips left mine… too soon for my liking. Before I could protest or lean in for more she tugged sharply at the shirt, yanking my head and hands backward and forcing my chin up.

Holly's teeth played across my neck, suckling, and biting at me as I swallowed hard.

Goosebumps rose as her free hand traced down my chest. She always loved to run her fingers over my muscles, feeling the cut between my pecs, my abs, and biceps. She walked a slow path with her fingernails over her favorite parts, like she was plotting a course across a map of treasured landmarks.

"Tell me what you want, Bobbie." She put her cheek right next to mine, whispering toward my ear. It was a pleasurable kind of hell to smell her, and feel her heat... feel her breath across my skin, but not be able to touch any part of her.

"Your mouth. Please."

I thought I could hear her smiling.

She released the shirt and slid it off of me the rest of the way.

"Is that all?"

"No, ma'am."

"What else do you want?"

I was studying her body intently. She watched me, watching her, and ran a hand down the hoodie she wore. Pulling the zipper down slowly as she went.

There was no shirt underneath. Just a simple black bra that lifted her beautiful breasts, adding extra perk that she really didn't need. She slid out of the hoodie, letting it fall to the floor behind her.

"Do you see what you want yet?"

I stared. My eyes lingered, then looked to her face.

"You want my mouth first."

"Yes."

She stepped forward and pressed me backwards to the bed. Holly's hunger was growing; her hands were getting rougher with me. The anticipation was getting to her as well. She dragged her nails down my chest, leaving red trails of fire that made me suck through my teeth.

It was a welcome pain.

A pain I deserved.

A long time coming…

And I wouldn't have anyone else give it to me. She dug her nails deep into my stomach and clutched deep, piercing me almost to the point of drawing blood. I grunted against the pain and felt my abs tremble.

"Stop?"

"No! …please." I closed my eyes.

She released me from her clutches anyway and I sighed at the release. It was bittersweet. Still, she wasted no time and moved down, quickly tearing at the buttons of my jeans and pulling them down.

Not all the way… just to my knees. Like I had done to her.

Panting with desire I wanted to beg her to do it, but Holly didn't tolerate begging. That would only result in her making me wait longer.

Her hand closed over the base of my cock, moving it around as she examined it from different angles. She made a soft sound, like a coo. Holly loved the size of it. It wasn't freakishly big, nothing that was deserving of a nickname.

But it was thick, above average, and she always enjoyed the opportunity to handle it.

"You're bigger than I remember. Are you excited?"

I was. I could almost feel it straining against its own skin. A response was coming up but before I could speak I felt her mouth close over me. She rolled her tongue slowly around it as she lowered her head and continued to swallow, drawing all of me in.

199

Slow inhale…

…slow exhale…

That wasn't working., and I had no control over my body as she started to rise and fall on me, sucking hungrily and squeezing as she pulled at the base.

My hand moved quickly to her hair, and I tried to get her to slow her pace. She must have read my cue.

I felt her lips come off at the base and suddenly felt her teeth close on me. Clenching in anticipation I moaned through a tight jaw as she slowly dragged her teeth back up the length of my cock.

The warm, wet feel of her mouth was suddenly gone, replaced by her hand slowly working me over. I lay there, breathing heavier, as she let go of me.

It didn't register immediately, but when I no longer felt her close to me I blinked. She delighted in teasing me.

Holly took great pleasure in working me close to a finish, then cutting me off.

I opened my eyes and lifted my head, watching her remove the last leg of her jeans.

In the growing darkness of the room, she walked closer. Her milky white skin and ample curves were almost glowing - a contrast against the shadows. She crawled over me and straddled my body, kissing me deeply.

My arms went around her, squeezing her tightly. Squeezing harder than she anticipated, but she didn't fight. was crushing her to me and she moaned loudly as our mouth met and danced together.

It was something I hadn't felt with Holly in a long time.

My hands pushed up through her hair, making my best effort to draw her into me. I felt safe, and protected, and whole in that moment.

Of all the things we had been through, I had never sought solace in her and I should have.

She moaned through the depths of our kisses, grinding her hips down on me. Her hand reach down between us but I caught her by the wrist. She pulled free of the kiss and looked at me a bit surprised.

"Not yet." I had to fight myself to stop her. I wanted nothing more than to be inside of her, but I knew I wouldn't last. Not with her.

Not with her body.

Certainly not with the way I know she can move.

"Lay down." I released her wrist and pushed against her shoulder. She slid off me to the side as she licked her lips.

"Yes, sir."

She crawled up as she lay down, stretching her body out with her arms over her head. I paused to appreciate the curvature of her ample but lithe frame as she curled her legs slightly. I slid up next to her and cupped her breast, squeezing gently.

A quiet sigh escaped her mouth and I felt her hips rise next to me. Her hand wrapped gently around the back of my head and she pulled – ever so slightly. She would submit to me, but you could never completely calm the fire in her.

Some women fear the fire. Over the years, Holly had become it.

201

I closed my mouth over her nipple, sucking and biting gently as my other hand moved slowly down between her legs. She spread her thighs for me, giving my fingers just enough space while still having to force their way down.

She liked to make me work for what I wanted.

My tongue swirled firm, deliberate circles around her nipple, my fingers testing the tightness of her pussy. She was wet… and her mouth parted in a long purr as I slid two fingers into her.

"God, Bobbie." Her back arched as I bit at her breast, working my fingers deep inside of her. I lavished her with attention, delivering nips of pain at her nipple while curling my fingers upward and using my thumb to press around her sweet spot.

Her hips bucked into my hand as I cupped her pussy tightly, pressing my fingers deep and practically lifting her. My fingers curled to hit that spot I knew would steal away her control.

It didn't take long.

She was practically crying and shaking.

I continued to roll my fingertips inside her, curled and pressing into her flesh, quickening the pace while adding force to each thrust.

Her nails dug into the back of my neck and she dragged her other hand across my shoulders, leaving what I knew would be lasting marks. The pain was bliss. I responded by sucking hard at her breast, driving my fingers deeper into her. I felt her body tense and stiffen, her muscles going taut. She arched her back again and was begging... though I couldn't tell if it was pleading for more or begging me to stop.

I felt her muscles clamp down on my fingers and I held them still. She froze, trembling and shaking, her thighs slamming shut on my hand like a trap. My tongue lapped her nipple once more with increased pressure before I relented.

Placing several soft kisses across her breast, I breathed in her scent once more before I sat up on my elbow.

Her chest was heaving, breasts rising and falling as she gulped for air, her body still shaking involuntarily. Holly slowly relaxed, her back settling to the bed, the death grip of her thighs relaxing.

"Oh... Bobbie." She exhaled sharply through pursed lips, opening her eyes to look at me, an eyebrow arching up one over the other. I just let a slow smile creep across my face. She moaned and turned her hips, pressing her ass into the bed.

When I saw that she had all but dissolved from the pleasure, and her trembling had settled, I slowly removed by fingers. She moaned out her gratitude, but also a complaint at the loss. She murmured up to me with a quiet whimper, "I need you inside me, Bobbie."

203

Her body was glistening in the little light that crept in through the window. She was quaking, and her beautiful golden curls were already a wild mess around her head. Her face was glowing as her eyes pleaded for me.

There was no way I would ever be able to deny her.

"Please," she begged in a hushed whisper.

"Yes, ma'am."

There was more passion in that moment than I had ever felt with her before, but I didn't let it overtake me. I rolled onto her slowly and used my knee to gently spread her thighs open, sliding myself between her legs.

She reached between us again, but I didn't stop her. Her hand gripped me firmly and guided it toward her, wrapping a leg up around my lower back and ass to pull me into her pussy.

Laying down, wanting to bathe in her, I buried my face in her neck and pressed deeper inside of her. We groaned in unison, making beautiful music like two finely tuned instruments that hadn't been played in ages.

My hand gripped her thigh, just below her ass, as I began to pump into her, slowly increasing my pace and the force of each thrust. She tried to contain her whimpers but was soon arching against me and moaning loudly, the occasional yelp of pain escaping her lips between moans that came deep from within.

I knew it was hurting her. I could feel how tight she was but she wouldn't let the pace slow. If I slowed, she bucked harder and pushed her hips into me.

There was no slowing or stopping.

There was no restraint allowed.

If I wouldn't give her what she wanted, she'd take it from me.

Her breasts bounced and slid beneath me as I gave her full, hard thrusts. Her nails cut into my back again as her body began to tense. She came again for me, her rapid moaning growing into guttural screams and shouts.

The angry grunts and lustful sounds rolling into my ear shook me to my core, and I couldn't contain myself.

My body seized and I fell into her as waves rolled over me. She could feel it rising in me and her legs wrapped tight as I tried to pull out of her. She drew my back in, forcing me deep as I gasped. I complied and dug in, my cock throbbing hard as I came in what felt like an endless and explosive climax.

I lost my senses. My vision blurred. I felt the room spin.

My arms gave as the last of my energy left me and I collapsed into her.

We lay there together, unable to move... or unwilling.

Holly inhaled sharply, her breathing ragged and rising against me. I wanted to consume her, like fire consumes every source of fuel.

"Kiss me," she whispered.

I managed to lift myself slowly, my own breaths coming to me in gulps. Sweat was running down my face, dripping from the tip of my nose.

She repeated herself, and I leaned down, pressing my lips to hers. Soft at first, then deeper. There was no intensive teasing or tongue play. It was just a long, slow, steady embrace as we breathed against one another.

Our lips came apart slowly and I touched my forehead to hers, my eyes closed.

"I love you," I said softly. "I never stopped… I just lost my way."

I opened my eyes to her and she was smiling weakly at me.

"I found you," she whispered.

*****

I watched her sleep next to me, curled under the bedspread and sheets. Her hair was a tangled mess, her cheeks were still flushed, and she lay there with her mouth open lightly snoring.

It lacked any grace, but I wouldn't expect anything else.

That was my Holly.

Sleep didn't come to me. That was all I had done in the hospital outside of sitting and watching Hunter.

If I ever had a sleep deficit, I was well caught up with energy to store.

I sat up and moved to the edge of the bed, rubbing my hands across the thighs of my pajama pants. Holly had bought these for me two years ago for Christmas. They were covered in bright yellow smiling emojis. I threw them on as a joke and we shared a little laugh over memories before she fell asleep.

Staring into the dark corner of the room, my thoughts went to Hunter again. I wondered if he might have woken, and what he would be thinking or feeling if he woke alone in a dark hospital room.

My hands went to the side table, picking up my zippo and cigarettes. Opening the pack, I plucked a cigarette and paused before putting it in my mouth.

Holly…

I put the cigarette back and tossed the pack and zippo down on the bed.

Moving quietly through the room, I stepped out into the hall and closed the bedroom door behind me. I needed a drink and didn't want to wake her – though by how quickly she passed out I imagined she was out cold for the night.

I tried to keep my footfalls light, but the hollow crawlspace made every step seem to echo like the house was built atop a canyon. I cursed under my breath and walked by the living room, steadying myself with the wall to try and keep my weight off my footsteps.

"Hey Bobbie."

I jumped sideways at the voice, putting my back to the wall and peering into the darkness of the living room. The light switched on, and I squinted against the light as it pierced my eyes.

Blake was sitting in my recliner.

My brow curled and I stepped into the room, still squinting a bit against the light.

"Blake, what are you doing here?"

"You told me to come by."

I shook my head at him and chuckled softly, responding in a hushed tone. "I didn't mean come by in the middle of the night. It's late."

"I know. I figured this was the best time."

"Not really." I thumbed over my shoulder. "I need to sleep. Come back tomorrow."

"No. This is good. I need you both here."

Blake stood up from the recliner and drew a pistol from the pocket of his hoodie. My hands went up as a wave of vertigo hit me. I stepped back and found the corner of the living room entry, bumping against it.

"Whoa… whoa… Blake. What are you doing?"

"What I've been trying to do. Take from you just like you took from me. But you're surprisingly versatile for an old fuck."

"I don't… why?" I struggled with the thought even though I knew in my mind exactly why.

He raised the pistol at me, his face twisting in anger and the barrel of the gun shook in his hand a little.

208

"You know why," he said through clenched teeth. "You took her from me. She was the only one who cared, the only one to notice, and you killed her."

Sarah.

My Sarah.

"Blake… listen…"

"Shut up!" He stepped toward me again, pushing the pistol in my direction. "You're a murderer. You stole the only thing I loved, and she loved me, too. You have no idea what that feels like."

"Blake, I lost her, too."

"*You killed her!*"

I flinched as he shouted at me, stepping closer and jabbing the gun toward me. All I could think about was Holly in the next room. As long as I was between him and her, and still standing, then she would be okay.

My hands stayed up, trying to put words together that would calm him but nothing came. I knew the rage that I had been wrestling with was almost uncontrollable. He seemed well beyond that point.

"I wanted you to know what it felt like, before it was your turn." He was trembling, the gun shaking in his hand. His finger was white knuckled on the trigger, and he was aiming dead on at near point blank range.

"I took the people you loved. My grandmother, who obviously cared more about you than anyone else." He stepped toward me again, his lip curling. "That stupid waitress… Sarah used to tell me how much you talked about her. I even got your partner."

209

"Hunter isn't dead." I said flatly, more for me and my own reassurance than for him.

"Not yet. But I wouldn't worry about that." He raised the gun, pointing it toward my face.

"Bobbie?" Holly stepped down the hall and my head snapped in her direction. Blake turned his attention, aiming the gun at her.

The sound of the gunshot was deafening in the house. My ears rang as I felt the pressure change. Holly grunted and bounced back against the wall, her body crumbling to the floor inside her robe.

I immediately jumped on Blake, grabbing the hand with the gun and shoving him backwards. The momentum carried us across the living room into the flat screen, rocking the entertainment center back into the wall as picture frames and other items crashed to the floor

I had a few inches on Blake and a lot more muscle, but he had youth on me. I struggled to keep the gun pointed away from me and took a punch to the side of the face. That one hit rocked my entire world and I nearly lost my footing. My head throbbed and I felt like I was going to throw up.

If I gave one inch though, we were dead. I wasn't losing Holly. I kept my grip on his right hand, pushing the gun away, and used my right to deliver a wide swing. It caught him in the temple and his knees buckled.

My fist swung again.

And again.

I lost count of the number of times I hit him, but he finally let go of the gun and fell to his back on the floor.

210

His face was bloodied and cut along his cheek and brow. Blood ran from his nose and mouth and he coughed and stirred on the floor. I picked up the gun and pointed it. I had no intention of using it. I stood there panting, trying to remember where I left my phone.

"You should... kill me. Like you killed her." He tried to sit up, lifting himself onto an elbow as he looked at me. "She moaned you know. Sarah. She moaned just like your wife when I fucked her. And now I killed her, to-"

I felt my finger squeeze the trigger.

The action repeated.

The report of the gunshot rang out again and again as the flash from the muzzle lit the remaining shadows of the room. I kept squeezing until the trigger froze, and the gun was empty.

Every round found its way into him – his chest, his face.

The front door came off its hinges and exploded inward shortly after the last bullet was fired. I didn't recognize them at first among the shouting and the bright flashlights.

It took me a moment to process the faces of Nick Farzo and his partner, Carter.

They had kicked in the door and came in with weapons drawn. Their posture loosened as they saw me standing there over Blake's body.

A cloud of smoke hung in the air from the gunshots, mingled with disturbed dust from the scuffle and forced entry.

They were talking to me, but it wasn't processing. I looked at the pistol in my hand, then to Blake, and I dropped the gun. I turned and bolted back to the hallway, dropping next to Holly.

Her robe was soaked in blood. I could hear her breathing, raspy, and labored.

"Holly. Holly! Holly, talk to me, baby." I moved her enough to lay her down on the floor. My instincts kicked in and I started checking her. Opening the robe, I could see it plain as day. She had a gunshot wound in her chest.

Nick was right next to me on his phone, calling for an ambulance. Holly blinked at me as her eyes fluttered. Her hand came up to me as she struggled to get a breath.

"I found us," she managed to choke out the words, just barely.

I looked to Nick, eyes locking with his. "Go in my bedroom closet. Get the jump bag." He moved with the speed of a wild cat, and my attention turned back to Holly. She was still looking at me.

Her breathing was getting more shallow, slower. I knew exactly what the problem was. It was the same wound that nearly claimed my patient last week, and it's what killed our daughter.

I wasn't losing Holly, too.

Nick slid next to me with the jump bag and I tore into it, pulling the contents out to retrieve the chest seal. I threw Nick the bag valve mask I kept in my personal gear and he quickly ripped the pouch open and assembled it.

212

I had the wound covered instantly. I only prayed that it wasn't worse than a collapsing lung, that the bullet hadn't done additional damage bouncing around in her rib cage. Rolling her to her side I slid my hand around behind her. It didn't take long to find a small clean exit wound.

Laying her back down, I grabbed the mask from Nick as he attached the small portable oxygen bottle to the tubing. It wasn't much, but it would be enough until the paramedics showed.

I hoped.

I used the bag valve mask to force air into her lungs, the chest seal fluttering slightly with each squeeze.

Her eyes were closed already, but I wasn't stopping.

"She's still got a pulse, Bobbie." Nick was checking her, drawing on his old training. He may have failed his paramedic tests repeatedly, but he always was a hell of a basic, and that little bit of extra might be exactly what it takes to save her.

"She's gonna be fine," I said through clenched teeth as I continued to breathe for her. I heard the sound of sirens climbing steadily in the distance.

"Hang on, baby. I got you."

*****

Nick sat with me in the waiting area of the ER.

Holly had been rushed back and I was forced to wait, impatient and on edge. They weren't really giving me anything yet, and I understood. They couldn't guarantee anything, so it was best to say nothing. Despite knowing that, I desperately wanted someone to just come to me and tell me she would be fine.

I knew she would be.

I needed them to say it.

Needed to hear it.

For the love of Christ, someone say it.

Nick and I didn't speak. He just sat with me, brought me coffee, and was a presence in the waiting area. He knew that's what I needed from him.

It felt like an eternity had passed, and I was losing my grip on self-control. I needed a distraction or I feared I'd barge through and check on her myself.

"Nick."

He raised his head, his eyebrows going up. He looked ridiculously out of place in that black mobster-style getup against the clean whites and greens of the hospital.

"Where the fuck did you guys come from?"

That had been bothering me since we got here, but the answer was low on my priority list while I struggled with worry and fear.

Nick hesitated to answer and put his hands up.

"We had your house wired while you were in the hospital, Bobbie. You were a suspect in two murders and Carter got a warrant to track and monitor."

214

"So, you heard everything then."

"Carter and I were on watch, posted about a block away. We heard what we needed to hear to move in but…."

"But I killed him."

"Bobbie, you protected yourself, and you saved Holly."

"I killed him, Nick."

"His decisions cost him his life, Bobbie. That's not on you."

"What about the oath to do no harm?"

Nick scoffed. "You can't buy into that Hippocratic oath shit right now, B. Do no harm? How are you gonna help anyone if you're dead. Don't be a fuckin' schmuck."

I lowered my head and sighed, wringing my hands together.

"That doesn't excuse what I did, Nick. I didn't have to kill him. You were right there."

"You didn't know that. It was self-defense, and that's exactly how we're writing it up.

"I need to know what the hell is going on." I changed the subject, standing and pacing a moment before walking to the information desk in the waiting area.

"Bobbie…" The technician looked at me, with all the patience in the world for someone who had already asked a thousand time, "as soon we know, the doctor will come see you."

My eyes closed in frustration. I wouldn't take it out on her. No matter how frustrated I was. I understood her position. I just nodded and turned to walk back. I paused when I heard the doors open in the waiting area.

215

The doc came out and walked straight toward me, looking calm and confident.

God please let it be okay.

"Bobbie, I hate seeing you under these circumstances." He extended a hand and I shook it limply.

"Is Holly alright?"

He smiled and patted my hand, his face wrinkling up a bit, showing his age – though his white hair did the same more effectively.

"She's just fine. The baby is fine, too."

"The what?" Nick and I both sputtered in stereo.

He grinned a knowing smile.

"I didn't think you knew. It's a bit early for congratulations, but given the circumstances I'd say it's needed. Your wife is pregnant, we confirmed it with her lab work."

"Holy shit, B!" Nick had taken up behind me. "Way to go!"

I felt a hard clap on my back that made me sway and struggled to find words. Tears started forming easily enough though.

Truthfully, I struggled to remember how to breathe.

"Can I see her?" I barely managed to choke out the request.

Nick laughed. "In about 9 months, B. She's gotta be born yet, eh?"

I could appreciate Nick's levity and spirit, but the teasing was lost on me at the moment. I just needed to see Holly awake.

"She's resting right now in recovery. Just a little longer and one of the nurses will come get you."

I nodded and started to turn away when the doctor caught my hand in another firm shake.

"Congratulations, son."

Epilogue

It wasn't easy walking the halls of the hospital without Hunter. It's not something I ever expected to happen, and even though more than a month had gone by it was still a major adjustment.

Every day was a painful crawl.

I hadn't been cleared back to work yet, and was still technically on disability until I finished the therapy and medical examinations after my concussion. Another couple weeks and I'd be fine.

Hunter would never share a truck with me again though. I would have to find a new partner.

I gave the nurses' station a pat with my hand as I walked up, continuing past it. The ladies all recognized me and gave me smiles. They had grown accustomed to seeing me daily, at almost the same time in the morning.

I almost always brought them coffee and donuts, or bagels.

There were no gifts today, I was too distracted.

Hunter was awake.

He had been awake already, but today was the first opportunity to talk to him without him being so heavily medicated. They had moved him out of ICU recently, and it looked like he may be getting discharged soon. I spoke with him on the phone this morning and let him know I was coming up.

Popping the latch on his room I opened the door and was startled by a nurse hurrying out. She nearly ran me over, her cheeks flushing as she made eye contact with me.

I stepped aside to let her go by and then looked in to see Hunter chilling in the recliner. His face lit with a wide grin when he saw me.

"Badger! You skeezy fuck."

He looked pretty good all things considered. He had some pigmentation issues where skin was healing differently around the side of his face and neck. His arms were still bandaged, and they told him he would likely have significant scarring.

Hunter didn't give a shit – he was actually kind of excited.

He already had a half-dozen bullshit stories about the scars he insisted were guaranteed to have him drowning in pussy.

"How you doin', buddy?" I walked around and sat on the edge of his bed across from him. He just smiled at me again and shook his head.

"Better than ever. I feel fantastic."

In the recent visits talking to Hunter, he was amazingly optimistic. I attributed it to being snowed on pain medications for the significant burns he had received. Now, even with fewer medications, he remained happier than a fly on shit.

He and I had talked about what happened already. I caught him up to speed, but I never addressed the death of our 3rd rider that he'd become so interested in. I wasn't sure how it would impact him. My thoughts compelled me to talk about it today though.

"Hunter… I'm sorry about Sara. All this shit wouldn't have happen-"

"Shuuuut the fuck uuuuup." He cut me off and swatted at the air. "Don't even start with that shit. It's cool, man."

He adjusted himself so he was sitting up more, reducing his slouch. He dug a finger into his eye, rubbing it as he squinted and continued to bat the topic back at me.

"We all have our own Sara in life, brother. Loss is all around us. People die. People come into our lives, and then they go out again. Sometimes we're the ones who leave. Am I right?"

I nodded to him and listened.

"Like you, baby. You lost your kid but you're gonna be a daddy again! And you're gonna be *so good*."

"How the fuck are you this happy all the time with the shit we've been through, Hunter?"

I was amazed. He never seemed to let shit get to him. I may have had more road experience, but I envied him for his chill outlook.

220

"Fuck… Bobbie… man, I fear. I feel. There are dark places I don't let my mind wander, and memories I don't dare unlock. Life ain't so good all the time in Hunter's brain." He tapped his head.

"Well, you do a solid job of hiding it."

"Nah… Bobbie, it's not about hiding it." He sat forward in the chair, sighing and adjusting himself as he winced and grunted softly. "It's all about happiness."

Hunter scratched as his cheek, wincing a bit as he bumped some of his bandages, then he looked to me through sage eyes with a warm smile.

"Happiness is glass-half-full shit, brother." He pointed a finger at me. "It's seeing it half full and being thankful, and seeing the empty part and asking yourself what you can do about it. If not, you ask yourself if you can accept it like it is."

"It's not about what the world gives you, it's about what you think of what the world gives you. Happiness is equal to, or greater than, the difference between the way you see the events and shit you go through, and your expectation of what life should be giving you. So, if life meets your expectations, then you're happy, right? Happiness is that feeling where it's like… I love the world like it is right now."

Hunter nodded as he spoke, staring off into the room and around at the floor as he waved his hand talking to me. I just listened, because it felt so fucking good to hear him talking.

"Look at me man. I'm fucked, I can't remember half the shit I learned because I was technically dead and shit. I'll be lucky if I can get a job as an instructor. I'm done on the road for sure. I could deal with it head on, or I could try to fill that void that's as big as your fucking penis."

He jabbed a finger at me and settled back into his chair.

"You start relying on distractions and fun, baby. Like partying with Hunter… all the sex, and pussy… and oh my God the titties… When shit gets sour, you party hard and make your brain not think about all that shit. You push it down. But once the fun is over, you still got that hole."

"As long as you're not thinking, and having fun, then you think you're happy. You suspended your unhappy thoughts. I don't do that, man. I deal with it. I don't hide shit with fun, Bobbie. You get me?"

I stared at him for a moment and we looked at each other.

"No. Not at all. How fucking high are you right now?"

He grinned big and his eyes squinted

"I got the nurse to give me an extra dose… and a blow job. I'm happy."

"No shit." I looked around the room and back to him just smiling at me. "I'm glad you're alright, Hunter."

"Shit, you can't kill me. I'm fucking Superman. Besides someone has to be around to help you raise that kid and be a real daddy."

"I'm looking forward to that." My heart felt full. Fuller than it had in a long time as I watched him.

"I'mma teach your kid how to fight, fuck, and… gimme another F word."

"Fuck you."

"I said that one already."

"You're such an asshole."

"Forever and ever, babe. Hey… let's play that fucking game again. Hit me with a state."

"Ohio." I grinned.

"Goddammit."

About the Author

Derek is a retired Emergency Medical Professional and has been a lover of telling stories his entire life, having made the transition from "filthy liar" to "sexy author" about the same time silver hairs started showing up in his face (and other places.)

In the early days, he attempted to write science fiction and high fantasy, but discovered it was more fun to write about people touching other people's tingle-places (smut is cool) while mixing in action, explosions, and plenty of WTF moments.

He's also a gamer, gym rat, snow hater (despite living in Michigan), life liver, stunt double for Hulk, and he considers himself to be aggressively unfancy.

Stalk him:
www.Facebook.com/authorderekadam

Twitter @tbaymedia

Instagram @authorderekadam

Coming Soon in the Motor City Universe

Due Soldati – Fall 2017
(Derek Adam & Jillian Elizabeth)

Carter Avery is a by-the-book detective for Detroit and surrounding Wayne County. Known for his cunning and eagle eyes on the crime scene, he's assigned to decipher a string of unusual murders that will test his skill, and that of his new partner, Nick Farzo. In a city wrought with political corruption and organized crime, these two white-knight detectives will stop at nothing to put the offenders behind bars.

That is, until an outside influence delivers an ultimatum to the city of Detroit on the eve of Devil's Night, where record number arson outbreaks plague the city annually. When entire fire crews start turning up dead, and the women closest to Nick and Carter come under fire, these two soldiers may have to loosen their moral code to put their target down.

Heart of the D – Coming Soon
(Derek Adam)

Brick Miller has cycled back from his deployment overseas as a military physician, taking up a position with Receiving's cardiology team. While struggling with a return to normal life, he also struggles with his moral code as he begins to fall for a patient who doesn't have long to live. Can he save her, and himself, as the city crumbles around them?

225

44249071R00131

Made in the USA
Middletown, DE
01 June 2017